Agatha Christie was born in Torquay and encouraged to write by Eden Phillpotts, the Devon playwright. In her first book, *The Mysterious Affair at Styles*, she created the now famous Belgian detective, Hercule Poirot, who is as popular as Conan Doyle's Sherlock Holmes. This was published in 1920, and her acknowledged masterpiece, *The Murder of Roger Ackroyd*, was published in 1926. She wrote over seventy-five detective novels, romantic novels under the pseudonym of Mary Westmacott, and many short stories and plays – including *The Mousetrap*, which is still running after more than thirty years. Several of her stories have been filmed, including *Ten Little Niggers*, *Witness for the Prosecution* and *Murder on the Orient Express*. Hercule Poirot finally died in *Curtain* which, although written twenty years earlier, was published just before Agatha Christie's death in 1976. She was married to Sir Max Mallowan, the well-known archaeologist, and was a Dame Commander of the Order of the British Empire.

Also by Agatha Christie
in Pan Books

Agatha Christie

Elephants Can Remember

Pan Books London and Sydney

To Molly Myers
in return for many kindnesses

First published 1972 by William Collins Sons & Co Ltd
This edition published 1983 by Pan Books Ltd,
Cavaye Place, London SW10 9PG
in association with William Collins Sons & Co Ltd
9 8 7 6 5
© Agatha Christie Mallowan 1972
ISBN 0 330 28165 8
Printed and bound in Great Britain by
Collins, Glasgow

CONTENTS

Chapter 1

A LITERARY LUNCHEON

Mrs Oliver looked at herself in the glass. She gave a brief, sideways look towards the clock on the mantelpiece, which she had some idea was twenty minutes slow. Then she resumed her study of her coiffure. The trouble with Mrs Oliver was – and she admitted it freely – that her styles of hairdressing were always being changed. She had tried almost everything in turn. A severe pompadour at one time, then a windswept style where you brushed back your locks to display an intellectual brow, at least she hoped the brow was intellectual. She had tried tightly arranged curls, she had tried a kind of artistic disarray. She had to admit that it did not matter very much today what her type of hairdressing was, because today she was going to do what she very seldom did, wear a hat.

On the top shelf of Mrs Oliver's wardrobe there reposed four hats. One was definitely allotted to weddings. When you went to a wedding, a hat was a 'must'. But even then Mrs Oliver kept two. One, in a round bandbox, was of feathers. It fitted closely to the head and stood up very well to sudden squalls of rain if they should overtake one unexpectedly as one passed from a car to the interior of the sacred edifice, or as so often nowadays, a registrar's office.

The other, and more elaborate, hat was definitely for attending a wedding held on a Saturday afternoon in summer. It had flowers and chiffon and a covering of yellow net attached with mimosa.

The other two hats on the shelf were of a more all-purpose character. One was what Mrs Oliver called her 'country house hat', made of tan felt suitable for wearing with tweeds of almost any pattern, with a becoming brim that you could turn up or turn down.

Mrs Oliver had a cashmere pullover for warmth and a thin pullover for hot days, either of which was suitable in colour to go with this. However, though the pullovers were frequently worn, the hat was practically never worn.

Because, really, why put on a hat just to go to the country and have a meal with your friends?

The fourth hat was the most expensive of the lot and it had extraordinarily durable advantages about it. Possibly, Mrs Oliver sometimes thought, because it was so expensive. It consisted of a kind of turban of various layers of contrasting velvets, all of rather becoming pastel shades which would go with anything.

Mrs Oliver paused in doubt and then called for assistance.

'Maria,' she said, then louder, 'Maria. Come here a minute.'

Maria came. She was used to being asked to give advice on what Mrs Oliver was thinking of wearing.

'Going to wear your lovely smart hat, are you?' said Maria.

'Yes,' said Mrs Oliver. 'I wanted to know whether you think it looks best this way or the other way round.'

Maria stood back and took a look.

'Well, that's back to front you're wearing it now, isn't it?'

'Yes, I know,' said Mrs Oliver. 'I know that quite well. But I thought somehow it looked better that way.'

'Oh, why should it?' said Maria.

'Well, it's meant, I suppose. But it's got to be meant by me as well as the shop that sold it,' said Mrs Oliver.

'Why do you think it's better the wrong way round?'

'Because you get that lovely shade of blue and the dark nigger brown, and I think that looks better than the other way which is green with the red and the chocolate colour.'

At this point Mrs Oliver removed the hat, put it on again and tried it wrong way round, right way round and sideways, which both she and Maria disapproved of.

'You can't have it the wide way. I mean, it's wrong for your face, isn't it? It'd be wrong for anyone's face.'

'No. That won't do. I think I'll have it the right way round, after all.'

'Well, I think it's safer always,' said Maria.

Mrs Oliver took off the hat. Maria assisted her to put on a well cut, thin woollen dress of a delicate puce colour, and helped her to adjust the hat.

'You look ever so smart,' said Maria.

That was what Mrs Oliver liked so much about Maria. If given the least excuse for saying so, she always approved and gave praise.

'Going to make a speech at the luncheon, are you?' Maria asked.

'A speech!' Mrs Oliver sounded horrified. 'No, of course not. You know I never make speeches.'

'Well, I thought they always did at these here literary luncheons. That's what you're going to, isn't it? Famous writers of 1973 – or whichever year it is we've got to now.'

'I don't need to make a speech,' said Mrs Oliver. 'Several other people who *like* doing it will be making speeches, and they are much better at it than I would be.'

'I'm sure you'd make a lovely speech if you put your mind to it,' said Maria, adjusting herself to the rôle of a tempter.

'No, I shouldn't,' said Mrs Oliver. 'I know what I can do and I know what I can't. I can't make speeches. I get all worried and nervy and I should probably stammer or say the same thing twice. I should not only feel silly, I should probably look silly. Now it's all right with words. You can write words down or speak them into a machine or dictate them. I can do things with words so long as I know it's not a speech I'm making.'

'Oh well. I hope everything'll go all right. But I'm sure it will. Quite a grand luncheon, isn't it?'

'Yes,' said Mrs Oliver, in a deeply depressed voice. 'Quite a grand luncheon.'

And why, she thought, but did not say, why on earth am I going to it? She searched her mind for a bit because she always really liked knowing what she was going to do instead of doing it first and wondering why she had done it afterwards.

'I suppose,' she said, again to herself and not to Maria, who had had to return rather hurriedly to the kitchen, summoned by a smell of overflowing jam which she happened to have on the stove, 'I wanted to see what it felt like. I'm always being asked to literary lunches or something like that and I never go.'

Mrs Oliver arrived at the last course of the grand luncheon with a sigh of satisfaction as she toyed with the remains of the meringue on her plate. She was particularly fond of meringues and it was a delicious last course in a very delicious luncheon. Nevertheless, when one reached middle age, one had to be careful with meringues. One's teeth? They looked all right, they had the great advantage that they could not ache, they were white and quite agreeable-looking – just like the real thing. But it was true enough that they were *not* real teeth. And teeth that were not real teeth – or so Mrs Oliver believed – were not really of high class material. Dogs, she had always understood, had teeth of real ivory, but human beings had teeth merely of bone. Or, she supposed, if they were false teeth, of plastic. Anyway, the point was that you mustn't get involved in some rather shame-making appearance, which false teeth might lead you into. Lettuce was a difficulty, and salted almonds, and such things as chocolates with hard centres, clinging caramels and the delicious stickiness and adherence of meringues. With a sigh of satisfaction, she dealt with the final mouthful. It had been a good lunch, a very good lunch.

Mrs Oliver was fond of her creature comforts. She had enjoyed the luncheon very much. She had enjoyed the company, too. The luncheon, which had been given to cele-brated female writers, had fortunately not been confined to female writers only. There had been other writers, and critics, and those who read books as well as those who wrote them. Mrs Oliver had sat between two very charming members of the male sex. Edwin Aubyn, whose poetry she always enjoyed, an extremely entertaining person who had had various entertaining experiences in his tours abroad, and various literary and personal adventures. Also he was interested in restaurants and food and they had talked very happily about food, and left the subject of literature aside.

Sir Wesley Kent, on her other side, had also been an agreeable luncheon companion. He had said very nice things about her books, and had had the tact to say things that did not make her feel embarrassed, which many people could do almost without trying. He had mentioned one or two reasons why he had liked one or other of her books, and they had been the right reasons, and therefore Mrs Oliver had thought favourably of him for that reason. Praise from men, Mrs Oliver thought to herself, is always acceptable. It was women who gushed. Some of the things that women wrote to her! Really! Not always women, of course. Some-times emotional young men from very far away countries. Only last week she had received a fan letter beginning 'Reading your book, I feel what a noble woman you must be.' After reading *The Second Goldfish* he had then gone off into an intense kind of literary ecstasy which was, Mrs

Oliver felt, completely unfitting. She was not unduly modest. She thought the detective stories she wrote were quite good of their kind. Some were not so good and some were much better than others. But there was no reason, so far as she could see, to make anyone think that she was a noble woman. She was a lucky woman who had established a happy knack of writing what quite a lot of people wanted to read. Wonderful luck that was, Mrs Oliver thought to herself.

Well, all things considered, she had got through this ordeal very well. She had quite enjoyed herself, talked to some nice people. Now they were moving to where coffee was being handed round and where you could change partners and chat with other people. This was the moment of danger, as Mrs Oliver knew well. This was now where other women would come and attack her. Attack her with fulsome praise, and where she always felt lamentably inefficient at giving the right answers because there weren't really any right answers that you could give. It went really rather like a travel book for going abroad with the right phrases.

Question: 'I *must* tell you how very fond I am of reading your books and how wonderful I think they are.'

Answer from flustered author, 'Well, that's very kind. I am so glad.'

'You must understand that I've been waiting to meet you for months. It really is wonderful.'

'Oh, it's very nice of you. Very nice indeed.'

It went on very much like that. Neither of you seemed to be able to talk about anything of outside interest. It had to be all about your books, or the other woman's books if you knew what her books were. You were in the literary web and you weren't good at this sort of stuff. Some people could do it, but Mrs Oliver was bitterly aware of not having the proper capacity. A foreign friend of hers had once put her, when she was staying at an embassy abroad, through a kind of course.

'I listen to you,' Albertina had said in her charming, low, foreign voice, 'I have listened to what you say to that young man who came from the newspaper to interview you. You have not got – no! you have not got the pride you should have in your work. You should say "Yes, I write well. I write better than anyone else who writes detective stories." '

'But I don't,' Mrs Oliver had said at that moment. 'I'm

not bad, but – '

'Ah, do not say "I don't" like that. You must say you *do*; even if you do not think you do, you ought to *say* you do.'

'I wish, Albertina,' said Mrs Oliver, 'that you could interview these journalists who come. You would do it so well. Can't you pretend to be me one day, and I'll listen behind the door?'

'Yes, I suppose I could do it. It would be rather fun. But they would know I was not you. They know your face. But you must say "Yes, yes, I know that I am better than anyone else." You must say that to everybody. They should know it. They should announce it. Oh yes – it is terrible to hear you sitting there and say things as though you *apologize* for what you are. It must not be like that.'

It had been rather, Mrs Oliver thought, as though she had been a budding actress trying to learn a part, and the director had found her hopelessly bad at taking direction. Well, anyway, there'd be not much difficulty here. There'd be a few waiting females when they all got up from the table. In fact, she could see one or two hovering already. That wouldn't matter much. She would go and smile and be nice and say 'So kind of you. I'm so pleased. One is so glad to know people like one's books.' All the stale old things. Rather as you put a hand into a box and took out some useful words already strung together like a necklace of beads. And then, before very long now, she could leave.

Her eyes went round the table because she might perhaps see some friends there as well as would-be admirers. Yes, she did see in the distance Maurine Grant, who was great fun. The moment came, the literary women and the attendant cavaliers who had also attended the lunch, rose. They streamed towards chairs, towards coffee tables, towards sofas, and confidential corners. The moment of peril, Mrs Oliver often thought of it to herself, though usually at cocktail and not literary parties because she seldom went to the latter. At any moment the danger might arise, as someone whom you did not remember but who remembered you, or someone whom you definitely did not want to talk to but whom you found you could not avoid. In this case it was the first dilemma that came to her. A large woman. Ample proportions, large white champing teeth. What in French could have been called *une femme formidable,* but who definitely had not only the French variety of being formidable, but the English one of being supremely bossy. Obviously she either knew Mrs Oliver, or was intent on making her acquaintance there and then. The last was how it happened to go.

'Oh, Mrs Oliver,' she said in a high-pitched voice. 'What a pleasure to meet you today. I have wanted to for so long. I simply adore your books. So does my son. And my husband used to insist on never travelling without at least two of your books. But come, do sit down. There are so many things I want to ask you about.'

Oh well, thought Mrs Oliver, not my favourite type of woman, this. But as well her as any other.

She allowed herself to be conducted in a firm way rather as a police officer might have done. She was taken to a settee for two across a corner, and her new friend accepted coffee and placed coffee before her also.

'There. Now we are settled. I don't suppose you know my name. I am Mrs Burton-Cox.'

'Oh yes,' said Mrs Oliver, embarrassed, as usual. Mrs Burton-Cox? Did she write books also? No, she couldn't really remember anything about her. But she seemed to have heard the name. A faint thought came to her. A book on politics, something like that? Not fiction, not fun, not crime. Perhaps a high-brow intellectual with political bias? That ought to be easy, Mrs Oliver thought with relief. I can just let her talk and say 'How interesting!' from time to time.

'You'll be very surprised, really, at what I'm going to say,' said Mrs Burton-Cox. 'But I have felt, from reading your books, how sympathetic you are, how much you understand of human nature. And I feel that if there is anyone who can give me an answer to the question I want to ask, you will be the one to do so.'

'I don't think, really . . .' said Mrs Oliver, trying to think of suitable words to say that she felt very uncertain of being able to rise to the heights demanded of her.

Mrs Burton-Cox dipped a lump of sugar in her coffee and crunched it in a rather carnivorous way, as though it was a bone. Ivory teeth, perhaps, thought Mrs Oliver vaguely. Ivory? Dogs had ivory, walruses had ivory and elephants had ivory, of course. Great big tusks of ivory. Mrs Burton-Cox was saying:

'Now the first thing I must ask you – I'm pretty sure I am right, though – you have a goddaughter, haven't you?

A goddaughter who's called Celia Ravenscroft?'

'Oh,' said Mrs Oliver, rather pleasurably surprised. She felt she could deal perhaps with a goddaughter. She had a good many goddaughters – and godsons, for that matter. There were times, she had to admit as the years were growing upon her, when she couldn't remember them all. She had done her duty in due course, one's duty being to send toys to your godchildren at Christmas in their early years, to visit them and their parents, or to have them visit you during the course of their upbringing, to take the boys out from school perhaps, and the girls also. And then, when the crowning days came, either the twenty-first birthday at which a godmother must do the right thing and let it be acknowledged to be done, and do it handsomely, or else marriage which entailed the same type of gift and a financial or other blessing. After that godchildren rather receded into the middle or far distance. They married or went abroad to foreign countries, foreign embassies, or taught in foreign schools or took up social projects. Anyway, they faded little by little out of your life. You were pleased to see them if they suddenly, as it were, floated up on the horizon again. But you had to remember to think when you had seen them last, whose daughters they were, what link had led to your being chosen as a godmother.

'Celia Ravenscroft,' said Mrs Oliver, doing her best. 'Yes, yes, of course. Yes, definitely.'

Not that any picture rose before her eyes of Celia Ravenscroft, not, that is, since a very early time. The christening. She'd gone to Celia's christening and had found a very nice Queen Anne silver strainer as a christening present. Very nice. Do nicely for straining milk and would also be the sort of thing a goddaughter could always sell for a nice little sum if she wanted ready money at any time. Yes, she remembered the strainer very well indeed. Queen Anne – Seventeen-eleven it had been. Britannia mark. How much easier it was to remember silver coffee-pots or strainers or christening mugs than it was the actual child.

'Yes,' she said, 'yes, of course. I'm afraid I haven't seen Celia for a very long time now.'

'Ah yes. She is, of course, a rather impulsive girl,' said Mrs Burton-Cox. 'I mean, she's changed her ideas very often. Of course, very intellectual, did very well at university, but – her political notions – I suppose all young people have political notions nowadays.'

'I'm afraid I don't deal much with politics,' said Mrs Oliver, to whom politics had always been anathema.

'You see, I'm going to confide in you. I'm going to tell you exactly what it is I want to know. I'm sure you won't mind. I've heard from so many people how kind you are, how willing always.'

I wonder if she's going to try and borrow money from me, thought Mrs Oliver, who had known many interviews that began with this kind of approach.

'You see, it is a matter of the greatest moment to me. Something that I really feel I *must* find out. Celia, you see, is going to marry – or thinks she is going to marry – my son, Desmond.'

'Oh, indeed!' said Mrs Oliver.

'At least, that is their idea at present. Of course, one has to know about people, and there's something I want very much to know. It's an extraordinary thing to ask anyone and I couldn't go – well, I mean, I couldn't very well go and ask a stranger, but I don't feel you are a stranger, dear Mrs Oliver.'

Mrs Oliver thought, I wish you did. She was getting nervous now. She wondered if Celia had had an illegitimate baby or was going to have an illegitimate baby, and whether she, Mrs Oliver, was supposed to know about it and give details. That would be very awkward. On the other hand, thought Mrs Oliver, I haven't seen her now for five or six years and she must be about twenty-five or -six, so it would be quite easy to say I don't know anything.

Mrs Burton-Cox leaned forward and breathed hard.

'I want you to tell me because I'm sure you must know or perhaps have a very good idea how it all came about. Did her mother kill her father or was it the father who killed the mother?'

Whatever Mrs Oliver had expected, it was certainly not that. She stared at Mrs Burton-Cox unbelievingly.

'But I don't –' She stopped. 'I – I can't understand. I mean – what reason –'

'Dear Mrs Oliver, you must *know* . . . I mean, such a famous case . . . Of course, I know it's a long time ago now, well, I suppose ten – twelve years at least, but it did cause a lot of attention at the time. I'm sure you'll remember, you *must* remember.'

Mrs Oliver's brain was working desperately. Celia was her goddaughter. That was quite true. Celia's mother –

15

yes, of course, Celia's mother had been Molly Preston Grey, who had been a friend of hers, though not a particularly intimate one, and of course she had married a man in the Army, yes – what was his name – Sir Something Ravenscroft. Or was he an ambassador? Extraordinary, one couldn't remember these things. She couldn't even remember whether she herself had been Molly's bridesmaid. She thought she had. Rather a smart wedding at the Guards Chapel or something like that. But one *did* forget so. And after that she hadn't met them for years – they'd been out somewhere – in the Middle East? In Persia? In Iraq? One time in Egypt? Malaya? Very occasionally, when they had been visiting England, she met them again. But they'd been like one of those photographs that one takes and looks at. One knows the people vaguely who are in it but it's so faded that you really can't recognize them or remember who they were. And she couldn't remember now whether Sir Something Ravenscroft and Lady Ravenscroft, born Molly Preston Grey, had entered much into her life. She didn't think so. But then . . . Mrs Burton-Cox was still looking at her. Looking at her as though disappointed in her lack of *savoir-faire,* her inability to remember what had evidently been a *cause célèbre.*

'Killed? You mean – an accident?'

'Oh no. Not an accident. In one of those houses by the sea. Cornwall, I think. Somewhere where there were rocks. Anyway, they had a house down there. And they were both found on the cliff there and they'd been shot, you know. But there was nothing really by which the police could tell whether the wife shot the husband and then shot herself, or whether the husband shot the wife and then shot himself. They went into the evidence of the – you know – of the bullets and the various things, but it was very difficult. They thought it might be a suicide pact and – I forget what the verdict was. Something – it could have been misadventure or something like that. But of course everyone knew it must have been *meant,* and there were a lot of stories that went about, of course, at the time – '

'Probably all invented ones,' said Mrs Oliver hopefully, trying to remember even one of the stories if she could.

'Well, maybe. Maybe. It's very hard to say, I know. There were tales of a quarrel either that day or before, there was some talk of another man, and then of course there was the usual talk about some other woman. And one never knows which way it was about. I think things were hushed up a good deal because General Ravenscroft's position was rather a high one, and I think it was said that he'd been in a nursing home that year, and he'd been very run down or something, and that he really didn't know what he was doing.'

'I'm really afraid,' said Mrs Oliver, speaking firmly, 'that I must say that I don't know anything about it. I do remember, now you mention it, that there was such a case, and I remember the names and that I knew the people, but I never knew what happened or anything at all about it. And I really don't think I have the least idea . . .'

And really, thought Mrs Oliver, wishing she was brave enough to say it, how on earth *you* have the impertinence to ask me such a thing I don't know.

'It's very important that I should know,' Mrs Burton-Cox said.

Her eyes, which were rather like hard marbles, started to snap.

'It's important, you see, because of my boy, my dear boy wanting to marry Celia.'

'I'm afraid I can't help you,' said Mrs Oliver. 'I've never heard anything.'

'But you *must* know,' said Mrs Burton-Cox. 'I mean, you write these wonderful stories, you know all about crime. You know who commits crimes and why they do it, and I'm sure that all sorts of people will tell you the story behind the story, as one so much thinks of these things.'

'I don't know anything,' said Mrs Oliver, in a voice which no longer held very much politeness, and definitely now spoke in tones of distaste.

'But you do see that really one doesn't know who to go to ask about it? I mean, one couldn't go to the police after all these years, and I don't suppose they'd tell you anyway because obviously they were trying to hush it up. But I feel it's important to get the *truth*.'

'I only write books,' said Mrs Oliver coldly. 'They are entirely fictional. I know nothing personally about crime and have no opinions on criminology. So I'm afraid I can't help you in *any* way.'

'But you could ask your goddaughter. You could ask Celia.'

'Ask Celia!' Mrs Oliver stared again. 'I don't see how I could do *that*. She was – why, I think she must have been quite a child when this tragedy happened.'

'Oh, I expect she knew all about it, though,' said Mrs Burton-Cox. 'Children always know everything. And she'd tell you. I'm sure she'd tell *you*.'

'You'd better ask her yourself, I should think,' said Mrs Oliver.

'I don't think I could really do that,' said Mrs Burton-Cox. 'I don't think, you know, that Desmond would like it. You know he's rather – well, he's rather touchy where Celia is concerned and I really don't think that – no – I'm sure she'd tell you.'

'I really shouldn't dream of asking her,' said Mrs Oliver. She made a pretence of looking at her watch. 'Oh dear,' she said, 'what a long time we've been over this delightful lunch. I must run now. I have a very important appointment. Goodbye, Mrs – er – Bedley-Cox, so sorry I can't help you but these things are rather delicate and – does it really make any difference anyway, from your point of view?'

'Oh, I think it makes *all* the difference.'

At that moment, a literary figure whom Mrs Oliver knew well drifted past. Mrs Oliver jumped up to catch her by the arm.

'Louise, my dear, how lovely to see you. I hadn't noticed you were here.'

'Oh, Ariadne, it's a long time since I've seen *you*. You've grown a lot thinner, haven't you?'

'What nice things you always say to me,' said Mrs Oliver, engaging her friend by the arm and retreating from the settee. 'I'm rushing away because I've got an appointment.'

'I suppose you got tied up with that awful woman, didn't you?' said her friend, looking over her shoulder at Mrs Burton-Cox.

'She was asking me the most extraordinary questions,' said Mrs Oliver.

'Oh. Didn't you know how to answer them?'

'No. They weren't any of my business anyway. I didn't know anything about them. Anyway, I wouldn't have wanted to answer them.'

'Was it about anything interesting?'

'I suppose,' said Mrs Oliver, letting a new idea come into her head, 'I suppose it might be interesting, only – '

'She's getting up to chase you,' said her friend. 'Come along. I'll see you get out and give you a lift to anywhere you want to go if you haven't got your car here.'

'I never take my car about in London, it's so awful to park.'

'I know it is. Absolutely deadly.'

Mrs Oliver made the proper goodbyes. Thanks, words of greatly expressed pleasure, and presently was being driven round a London square.

'Eaton Terrace, isn't it?' said the kindly friend.

'Yes,' said Mrs Oliver, 'but where I've got to go now is – I think it's Whitefriars Mansions. I can't quite remember the name of it, but I know where it is.'

'Oh, flats. Rather modern ones. Very square and geometrical.'

'That's right,' said Mrs Oliver.

Chapter 2

FIRST MENTION OF ELEPHANTS

Having failed to find her friend Hercule Poirot at home, Mrs Oliver had to resort to a telephone enquiry.

'Are you by any chance going to be at home this evening?' asked Mrs Oliver.

She sat by her telephone, her fingers tapping rather nervously on the table.

'Would that be – ?'

'Ariadne Oliver,' said Mrs Oliver, who was always surprised to find she had to give her name because she always expected all her friends to know her voice as soon as they heard it.

'Yes, I shall be at home all this evening. Does that mean that I may have the pleasure of a visit from you?'

'It's very nice of you to put it that way,' said Mrs Oliver. 'I don't know that it will be such a pleasure.'

'It is always a pleasure to see you, *chère Madame*.'

'I don't know,' said Mrs Oliver. 'I might be going to – well, bother you rather. Ask things. I want to know what you think about something.'

'That I am always ready to tell anyone,' said Poirot.

'Something's come up,' said Mrs Oliver. 'Something tiresome and I don't know what to do about it.'

'And so you will come and see me. I am flattered. Highly flattered.'

'What time would suit you?' said Mrs Oliver.

'Nine o'clock? We will drink coffee together, perhaps, unless you prefer a Grenadine or a *Sirop de Cassis*. But no, you do not like that. I remember.'

'George,' said Poirot, to his invaluable manservant, 'we are to receive tonight the pleasure of a visit from Mrs Oliver. Coffee, I think, and perhaps a liqueur of some kind. I am never sure what she likes.'

'I have seen her drink kirsch, sir.'

'And also, I think, *crème de menthe*. But kirsch, I think, is what she prefers. Very well then,' said Poirot. 'So be it.'

Mrs Oliver came punctual to time. Poirot had been wondering, while eating his dinner, what it was that was driving Mrs Oliver to visit him, and why she was so doubtful about what she was doing. Was she bringing him some difficult problem, or was she acquainting him with a crime? As Poirot knew well, it could be anything with Mrs Oliver. The most commonplace things or the most extraordinary things. They were, as you might say, all alike to her. She was worried, he thought. Ah well, Hercule Poirot thought to himself, he could deal with Mrs Oliver. He always had been able to deal with Mrs Oliver. On occasion she maddened him. At the same time he was really very much attached to her. They had shared many experiences and experiments together. He had read something about her in the paper only that morning – or was it the evening paper? He must try and remember it before she came. He had just done so when she was announced.

She came into the room and Poirot deduced at once that his diagnosis of worry was true enough. Her hair-do, which was fairly elaborate, had been ruffled by the fact that she had been running her fingers through it in the frenzied and feverish way that she did sometimes. He received her with every sign of pleasure, established her in a chair, poured her some coffee and handed her a glass of kirsch.

'Ah!' said Mrs Oliver, with the sigh of someone who has relief. 'I expect you're going to think I'm awfully silly, but still . . .'

'I see, or rather, I saw in the paper that you were attending a literary luncheon today. Famous women writers. Something of that kind. I thought you never did that kind of thing.'

'I don't usually,' said Mrs Oliver, 'and I shan't ever do it again.'

'Ah. You suffered much?' Poirot was quite sympathetic. He knew Mrs Oliver's embarrassing moments. Extravagant praise of her books always upset her highly because, as she had once told him, she never knew the proper answers.

'You did not enjoy it?'

'Up to a point I did,' said Mrs Oliver, 'and then something very tiresome happened.'

'Ah. And that is what you have come to see me about.'

'Yes, but I really don't know why. I mean, it's nothing to do with you and I don't think it's the sort of thing you'd even be interested in. And I'm not really interested in it. At least, I suppose I must be or I wouldn't have wanted to come to you to know what you thought. To know what — well, what you'd do if you were me.'

'That is a very difficult question, that last one,' said Poirot. 'I know how I, Hercule Poirot, would act in anything, but I do not know how you would act, well though I know you.'

'You must have some idea by this time,' said Mrs Oliver. 'You've known me long enough.'

'About what — twenty years now?'

'Oh, I don't know. I can never remember what years are, what dates are. You know, I get mixed up. I know 1939 because that's when the war started and I know other dates because of queer things, here and there.'

'Anyway, you went to your literary luncheon. And you did not enjoy it very much.'

'I enjoyed the lunch but it was afterwards . . .'

'People said things to you,' said Poirot, with the kindliness of a doctor demanding symptoms.

'Well, they were just getting ready to say things to me. Suddenly one of those large, bossy women who always manage to dominate everyone and who can make you feel more uncomfortable than anyone else, descended on me. You know, like somebody who catches a butterfly or something, only she'd have needed a butterfly-net. She sort of rounded me up and pushed me on to a settee and then she began to talk to me, starting about a goddaughter of mine.'

'Ah yes. A goddaughter you are fond of?'

'I haven't seen her for a good many years,' said Mrs Oliver, 'I can't keep up with all of them, I mean. And then she asked me a most worrying question. She wanted me – oh dear, how very difficult it is for me to tell this – '

'No, it isn't,' said Poirot kindly. 'It is quite easy. Everyone tells everything to me sooner or later. I'm only a foreigner, you see, so it does not matter. It is easy because I am a foreigner.'

'Well, it is rather easy to say things to you,' said Mrs Oliver. 'You see, she asked me about the girl's father and mother. She asked me whether her mother had killed her father or her father had killed her mother.'

'I beg your pardon,' said Poirot.

'Oh, I know it sounds mad. Well, I thought it was mad.'

'Whether your goddaughter's mother had killed her father, or whether her father had killed her mother.'

'That's right,' said Mrs Oliver.

'But – was that a matter of fact? Had her father killed her mother or her mother killed her father?'

'Well, they were both found shot,' said Mrs Oliver. 'On the top of a cliff. I can't remember if it was in Cornwall or in Corsica. Something like that.'

'Then it was true, then, what she said?'

'Oh yes, that part of it was true. It happened years ago. Well, but I mean – why come to me?'

'All because you were a crime writer,' said Poirot. 'She no doubt said you knew all about crime. This was a real thing that happened?'

'Oh yes. It wasn't something like what would A do – or what would be the proper procedure if your mother had killed your father or your father had killed your mother. No, it was something that really happened. I suppose really I'd better tell you all about it. I mean, I can't remember all about it but it was quite well known at the time. It was about – oh, I should think it was about twelve years ago at least. And, as I say, I can remember the names of the people because I did know them. The wife had been at school with me and I'd known her quite well. We'd been friends. It was a well-known case – you know, it was in all the papers and things like that. Sir Alistair Ravenscroft and Lady Ravenscroft. A very happy couple and he was a colonel or a general and she'd been with him and they'd been all over the world. Then they bought this house somewhere –

I think it was abroad but I can't remember. And then there were suddenly accounts of this case in the papers. Whether somebody else had killed them or whether they'd been assassinated or something, or whether they killed each other. I think it was a revolver that had been in the house for ages and – well, I'd better tell you as much as I can remember.'

Pulling herself slightly together, Mrs Oliver managed to give Poirot a more or less clear *résumé* of what she had been told. Poirot from time to time checked on a point here or there.

'But why?' he said finally, 'why should this woman want to know this?'

'Well, that's what I want to find out,' said Mrs Oliver. 'I could get hold of Celia, I think. I mean, she still lives in London. Or perhaps it's Cambridge she lives in, or Oxford – I think she's got a degree and either lectures here or teaches somewhere, or does something like that. And – very modern, you know. Goes about with long-haired people in queer clothes. I don't think she takes drugs. She's quite all right and – just very occasionally I hear from her. I mean, she sends a card at Christmas and things like that. Well, one doesn't think of one's godchildren all the time, and she's quite twenty-five or -six.'

'Not married?'

'No. Apparently she is going to marry – or that is the idea – Mrs – What's the name of that woman again? – oh yes, Mrs Brittle – no – Burton-Cox's son.'

'And Mrs Burton-Cox does not want her son to marry this girl because her father killed her mother or her mother killed her father?'

'Well, I suppose so,' said Mrs Oliver. 'It's the only thing I can think. But what does it matter which? If one of your parents killed the other, would it really matter to the mother of the boy you were going to marry, which way round it was?'

'That is a thing one might have to think about,' said Poirot. 'It is – yes, you know it is quite interesting. I do not mean it is very interesting about Sir Alistair Ravenscroft or Lady Ravenscroft. I seem to remember vaguely – oh, some case like this one, or it might not have been the same one. But it is very strange about Mrs Burton-Cox. Perhaps she is a bit touched in the head. Is she very fond of her son?'

'Probably,' said Mrs Oliver. 'Probably she doesn't want him to marry this girl at all.'

'Because she may have inherited a predisposition to murder the man she marries – or something of that kind?'

'How do I know?' said Mrs Oliver. 'She seems to think that I can tell her, and she's really not told *me* enough, has she? But why, do you think? What's behind it all? What does it *mean*?'

'It would be almost interesting to find out,' said Poirot.

'Well, that's why I've come to you,' said Mrs Oliver. 'You like finding out things. Things that you can't see the reason for at first. I mean, that nobody can see the reason for.'

'Do you think Mrs Burton-Cox has any preference?' said Poirot.

'You mean that she'd rather the husband killed the wife, or the wife killed the husband? I don't think so.'

'Well,' said Poirot, 'I see your dilemma. It is very intriguing. You come home from a party. You've been asked to do something that is very difficult, almost impossible, and – you wonder what is the proper way to deal with such a thing.'

'Well, what would you think is the proper way?' said Mrs Oliver.

'It is not easy for me to say,' said Poirot. 'I'm not a woman. A woman whom you do not really know, whom you had met at a party, has put this problem to you, asked you to do it, giving no discernible reason.'

'Right,' said Mrs Oliver. 'Now what does Ariadne do? What does A do, in other words, if you were reading this as a problem in a newspaper?'

'Well, I suppose,' said Poirot, 'there are three things that A could do. A could write a note to Mrs Burton-Cox and say, "I'm very sorry but I really feel I cannot oblige you in this matter," or whatever words you like to put. B. You get into touch with your goddaughter and you tell her what has been asked of you by the mother of the boy, or the young man, or whatever he is, whom she is thinking of marrying. You will find out from her if she is really thinking of marrying this young man. If so, whether she has any idea or whether the young man has said anything to her about what his mother has got in her head. And there will be other interesting points, like finding out what this girl thinks of the mother of the young man she wants to marry. The third thing you could do,' said Poirot, 'and this really is what I firmly advise you to do, is . . .'

'I know,' said Mrs Oliver, 'one word.'

'Nothing,' said Poirot.

'Exactly,' said Mrs Oliver. 'I know that is the simple and proper thing to do. Nothing. It's darned cheek to go and tell a girl who's my goddaughter what her future mother-in-law is going about saying, and asking people. But –'

'I know,' said Poirot, 'it is human curiosity.'

'I want to know why that odious woman came and said what she did to me,' said Mrs Oliver. 'Once I know that I could relax and forget all about it. But until I know that . . .'

'Yes,' said Poirot, 'you won't sleep. You'll wake up in the night and, if I know you, you will have the most extraordinary and extravagant ideas which presently, probably, you will be able to make into a most attractive crime story. A whodunit – a thriller. All sorts of things.'

'Well, I suppose I could if I thought of it that way,' said Mrs Oliver. Her eyes flashed slightly.

'Leave it alone,' said Poirot. 'It will be a very difficult plot to undertake. It seems as though there could be no good reason for this.'

'But I'd like to make *sure* that there *is* no good reason.'

'Human curiosity,' said Poirot. 'Such a very interesting thing.' He sighed. 'To think what we owe to it throughout history. Curiosity. I don't know who invented curiosity. It is said to be usually associated with the cat. Curiosity killed the cat. But I should say really that the Greeks were the inventors of curiosity. They wanted to *know*. Before them, as far as I can see, nobody wanted to know *much*. They just wanted to know what the rules of the country they were living in were, and how they could avoid having their heads cut off or being impaled on spikes or something disagreeable happening to them. But they either obeyed or disobeyed. They didn't want to know *why*. But since then a lot of people have wanted to know *why* and all sorts of things have happened because of that. Boats, trains, flying machines and atom bombs and penicillin and cures for various illnesses. A little boy watches his mother's kettle raising its lid because of the steam. And the next thing we know is we have railway trains, leading on in due course to railway strikes and all that. And so on and so on.'

'Just tell me,' said Mrs Oliver, 'do you think I'm a terrible nosey-parker?'

'No, I don't,' said Poirot. 'On the whole I don't think

you are a woman of great curiosity. But I can quite see you getting in a het-up state at a literary party, busy defending yourself against too much kindness, too much praise. You ran yourself instead into a very awkward dilemma, and took a very strong dislike to the person who ran you into it.'

'Yes. She's a very tiresome woman, a very disagreeable woman.'

'This murder in the past of this husband and wife who were supposed to get on well together and no apparent signs of a quarrel was known. One never really read about any cause for it, according to you?'

'They were shot. Yes, they were shot. It could have been a suicide pact. I think the police thought it was at first. Of course, one can't find out about things all those years afterwards.'

'Oh yes,' said Poirot, 'I think I could find out something about it.'

'You mean – through the exciting friends you've got?'

'Well, I wouldn't say the exciting friends, perhaps. Certainly there are knowledgeable friends, friends who could get certain records, look up the accounts that were given of the crime at the time, some access I could get to certain records.'

'You could find out things,' said Mrs Oliver hopefully, 'and then tell me.'

'Yes,' said Poirot, 'I think I could help you to know at any rate the full facts of the case. It'll take a little time, though.'

'I can see that if you do that, which is what I want you to do, *I've* got to do something myself. I'll have to see the girl. I've got to see whether she knows anything about all this, ask her if she'd like me to give her mother-in-law-to-be a raspberry or whether there is any other way in which I can help her. And I'd like to see the boy she's going to marry, too.'

'Quite right,' said Poirot. 'Excellent.'

'And I suppose,' said Mrs Oliver, 'there might be people –' She broke off, frowning.

'I don't suppose people will be very much good,' said Hercule Poirot. 'This is an affair of the past. A *cause célèbre* perhaps at the time. But what is a *cause célèbre* when you come to think of it? Unless it comes to an astonishing *dénouement,* which this one didn't. Nobody remembers it.'

'No,' said Mrs Oliver, 'that is quite true. There was a lot about it in the papers and mentions of it for some time, and then it just – faded out. Well, like things do now. Like that girl, the other day. You know, who left her home and they couldn't find her anywhere. Well, I mean, that was five or six years ago and then suddenly a little boy, playing about in a sand heap or a gravel pit or something, suddenly came across her dead body. Five or six years later.'

'That is true,' said Poirot. 'And it is true that knowing from that body how long it is since death and what happened on the particular day and going back over various events of which there is a written record, one may in the end turn up a murderer. But it will be more difficult in your problem since it seems the answer must be one of two things: that the husband disliked his wife and wanted to get rid of her, or that the wife hated her husband or else had a lover. Therefore, it might have been a passionate crime or something quite different. Anyway, there would be nothing, as it were, to find out about it. If the police could not find out at the time, then the motive must have been a difficult one, not easy to see. Therefore it has remained a nine days' wonder, that is all.'

'I suppose I can go to the daughter. Perhaps that is what that odious woman was getting me to do – wanted me to do. She thought the daughter knew – well, the daughter might have known,' said Mrs Oliver. 'Children do, you know. They know the most extraordinary things.'

'Have you any idea how old this goddaughter of yours would have been at the time?'

'Well, I have if I reckon it up, but I can't say off-hand. I think she might have been nine or ten, but perhaps older, I don't know. I think that she was away at school at the time. But that may be just my fancy, remembering back what I read.'

'But you think Mrs Burton-Cox's wish was to make you get information from the daughter? Perhaps the daughter knows something, perhaps she said something to the son, and the son said something to his mother. I expect Mrs Burton-Cox tried to question the girl herself and got rebuffed, but thought the famous Mrs Oliver, being both a godmother and also full of criminal knowledge, might obtain information. Though why it should matter to her, I still don't see,' said Poirot. 'And it does not seem to me that what

you call vaguely "people" can help after all this time.'
He added, 'Would anybody remember?'

'Well, that's where I think they might,' said Mrs Oliver.

'You surprise me,' said Poirot, looking at her with a
somewhat puzzled face. '*Do* people remember?'

'Well,' said Mrs Oliver, 'I was really thinking of elephants.'
'Elephants?'

As he had thought often before, Poirot thought that
really Mrs Oliver was the most unaccountable woman. Why
suddenly elephants?

'I was thinking of elephants at the lunch yesterday,'
said Mrs Oliver.

'Why were you thinking of elephants?' said Poirot, with
some curiosity.

'Well, I was really thinking of teeth. You know, things
one tries to eat, and if you've got some sort of false teeth –
well, you can't do it very well. You know, you've got to
know what you can eat and what you can't.'

'Ah!' said Poirot, with a deep sigh. 'Yes, yes. The dentists,
they can do much for you, but not everything.'

'Quite so. And then I thought of – you know – our teeth
being only bone and so not awfully good, and how nice
it would be to be a dog, who has real ivory teeth. And then
I thought of anyone else who has ivory teeth, and I thought
about walruses and – oh, other things like that. And I
thought about elephants. Of course when you think of ivory
you do think of elephants, don't you? Great big elephant
tusks.'

'That is very true,' said Poirot, still not seeing the point
of what Mrs Oliver was saying.

'So I thought that what we've really got to do is to get
at the people who are like elephants. Because elephants,
so they say, don't forget.'

'I have heard the phrase, yes,' said Poirot.

'Elephants don't forget,' said Mrs Oliver. 'You know, a
story children get brought up on? How someone, an Indian
tailor, stuck a needle or something in an elephant's tusk.
No. Not a tusk, his trunk, of course, an elephant's trunk.
And the next time the elephant came past he had a great
mouthful of water and he splashed it out all over the tailor
though he hadn't seen him for several years. He hadn't forgotten. He remembered. That's the point, you see. Elephants
remember. What I've got to do is – I've got to get in touch
with some elephants.'

'I do not know yet if I quite see what you mean,' said Hercule Poirot. 'Who are you classifying as elephants? You sound as though you were going for information to the Zoo.'

'Well, it's not exactly like that,' said Mrs Oliver. 'Not elephants, as elephants, but the way people up to a point would resemble elephants. There are some people who *do* remember. In fact, one does remember queer things. I mean there are a lot of things that *I* remember very well. They happened – I remember a birthday party I had when I was five, and a pink cake – a lovely pink cake. It had a sugar bird on it. And I remember the day my canary flew away and I cried. And I remember another day when I went into a field and there was a bull there and somebody said it would gore me, and I was terrified and wanted to run out of the field. Well, I remember that quite well. It was a Tuesday too. I don't know why I should remember it was a Tuesday, but it was a Tuesday. And I remember a wonderful picnic with blackberries. I remember getting pricked terribly, but getting more blackberries than anyone else. It was wonderful! By that time I was nine, I think. But one needn't go back as far as that. I mean, I've been to hundreds of weddings in my life, but when I look back on a wedding there are only two that I remember *particularly*. One where I was a bridesmaid. It took place in the New Forest, I remember, and I can't remember who was there actually. I think it was a cousin of mine getting married. I didn't know her very well but she wanted a good many bridesmaids and, well, I came in handy, I suppose. But I know another wedding. That was a friend of mine in the Navy. He was nearly drowned in a submarine, and then he was saved, and then the girl he was engaged to, her people didn't want her to marry him but then he did marry her after that and I was one of her bridesmaids at the marriage. Well, I mean, there's always things you *do* remember.'

'I see your point,' said Poirot. 'I find it interesting. So you will go *à la recherche des éléphants*?'

'That's right. I'd have to get the date right.'

'There,' said Poirot, 'I hope I may be able to help you.'

'And then I'll think of people I knew about at that time, people that I may have known who also knew the same friends that I did, who probably knew General What-not. People who may have known them abroad, but whom I also knew although I mayn't have seen them for a good many years. You can look up people, you know, that you haven't seen for a long time. Because people are always quite pleased to see someone coming up out of the past, even if they can't remember very much about you. And then you naturally will talk about the things that were happening at that date, that you remember about.'

'Very interesting,' said Poirot. 'I think you are very well equipped for what you propose to do. People who knew the Ravenscrofts either well or not very well; people who lived in the same part of the world where the thing happened or who might have been staying there. More difficult, but I think one could get at it. And so, somehow or other one would try different things. Start a little talk going about what happened, what they think happened, what anyone else has ever told you about what might have happened. About any love-affairs the husband or wife had, about any money that somebody might have inherited. I think you could scratch up a lot of things.'

'Oh dear,' said Mrs Oliver, 'I'm afraid really I'm just a nosey-parker.'

'You've been given an assignment,' said Poirot, 'not by someone you like, not by someone you wish to oblige, but someone you entirely dislike. That does not matter. You are still on a quest, a quest of knowledge. You take your own path. It is the path of the elephants. The elephants *may* remember. *Bon voyage*,' said Poirot.

'I beg your pardon,' said Mrs Oliver.

'I'm sending you forth on your voyage of discovery,' said Poirot. '*A la recherche des éléphants*.'

'I expect I'm mad,' said Mrs Oliver sadly. She brushed her hands through her hair again so that she looked like the old picture books of Struwelpeter. 'I was just thinking of starting a story about a Golden Retriever. But it wasn't going well. I couldn't get started, if you know what I mean.'

'All right, abandon the Golden Retriever. Concern yourself only with elephants.'

BOOK 1

Elephants

Chapter 3

GREAT AUNT ALICE'S GUIDE TO KNOWLEDGE

'Can you find my address book for me, Miss Livingstone?'

'It's on your desk, Mrs Oliver. In the left-hand corner.'

'I don't mean that one,' said Mrs Oliver. 'That's the one I'm using now. I mean my last one. The one I had last year, or perhaps the one before that again.'

'Has it been thrown away, perhaps?' suggested Miss Livingstone.

'No, I don't throw away address books and things like that because so often you want one. I mean some address that you haven't copied into the new one. I expect it may be in one of the drawers of the tallboys.'

Miss Livingstone was a fairly new arrival, replacing Miss Sedgwick. Ariadne Oliver missed Miss Sedgwick. Sedgwick knew so many things. She knew the places where Mrs Oliver sometimes put things, the kind of places Mrs Oliver kept things in. She remembered the names of people Mrs Oliver had written nice letters to, and the names of people that Mrs Oliver, goaded beyond endurance, had written rather rude things to. She was invaluable, or rather, had been invaluable. 'She was like – what was the book called?' Mrs Oliver said, casting her mind back. 'Oh yes, I know – a big brown book. All Victorians had it. *Enquire Within Upon Everything*. And you could too! How to take iron mark stains off linen, how to deal with curdled mayonnaise, how to start a chatty letter to a bishop. Many, many things. It was all there in *Enquire Within Upon Everything*.' Great Aunt Alice's great standby.

Miss Sedgwick had been just as good as Aunt Alice's

book. Miss Livingstone was not at all the same thing. Miss Livingstone stood there always, very long-faced with a sallow skin, looking purposefully efficient. Every line of her face said 'I am very efficient.' But she wasn't really, Mrs Oliver thought. She only knew all the places where former literary employers of hers had kept things and where she clearly considered Mrs Oliver ought to keep them.

'What I want,' said Mrs Oliver, with firmness and the determination of a spoilt child, 'is my 1970 address book. And I think 1969 as well. Please look for it as quick as you can, will you?'

'Of course, of course,' said Miss Livingstone.

She looked round her with the rather vacant expression of someone who is looking for something she has never heard of before but which efficiency may be able to produce by some unexpected turn of luck.

If I don't get Sedgwick back, I shall go mad, thought Mrs Oliver to herself. I can't deal with this thing if I don't have Sedgwick.

Miss Livingstone started pulling open various drawers in the furniture in Mrs Oliver's so-called study and writing-room.

'Here is last year's,' said Miss Livingstone happily. 'That will be much more up-to-date, won't it? 1971.'

'I don't want 1971,' said Mrs Oliver.

Vague thoughts and memories came to her.

'Look in that tea-caddy table,' she said.

Miss Livingstone looked round, looking worried.

'That table,' said Mrs Oliver, pointing.

'A desk book wouldn't be likely to be in a tea-caddy,' said Miss Livingstone, pointing out to her employer the general facts of life.

'Yes, it could,' said Mrs Oliver. 'I seem to remember.'

Edging Miss Livingstone aside, she went to the tea-caddy table, raised the lid, looked at the attractive inlaid work inside. 'And it *is* here,' said Mrs Oliver, raising the lid of a papier-mâché round canister, devised to contain Lapsang Souchong as opposed to Indian tea, and taking out a curled-up small brown notebook.

'Here it is,' she said.

'That's only 1968, Mrs Oliver. Four years ago.'

'That's about right,' said Mrs Oliver, seizing it and taking it back to the desk. 'That's all for the present, Miss Livingstone, but you might see if you can find my birthday book somewhere.'

'I didn't know . . .'

'I don't use it now,' said Mrs Oliver, 'but I used to have one once. Quite a big one, you know. Started when I was a child. Goes on for years. I expect it'll be in the attic upstairs. You know, the one we use as a spare room sometimes when it's only boys coming for holidays, or people who don't mind. The sort of chest or bureau thing next to the bed.'

'Oh. Shall I look and see?'

'That's the idea,' said Mrs Oliver.

She cheered up a little as Miss Livingstone went out of the room. Mrs Oliver shut the door firmly behind her, went back to the desk and started looking down the addresses written in faded ink and smelling of tea.

'Ravenscroft. Celia Ravenscroft. Yes. 14 Fishacre Mews, S.W.3. That's the Chelsea address. She was living there then. But there was another one after that. Somewhere like Strand-on-the-Green near Kew Bridge.'

She turned a few more pages.

'Oh yes, this seems to be a later one. Mardyke Grove. That's off Fulham Road, I think. Somewhere like that. Has she got a telephone number? It's very rubbed out, but I think – yes, I think that's right – Flaxman . . . Anyway, I'll try it.'

She went across to the telephone. The door opened and Miss Livingstone looked in.

'Do you think that perhaps –'

'I found the address I want,' said Mrs Oliver. 'Go on looking for that birthday book. It's important.'

'Do you think you could have left it when you were in Sealy House?'

'No, I don't,' said Mrs Oliver. 'Go on looking.'

She murmured, as the door closed, 'Be as long as you like about it.'

She dialled the telephone and waited, opening the door to call up the stairs: 'You might try that Spanish chest. You know, the one that's bound with brass. I've forgotten where it is now. Under the table in the hall, I think.'

Mrs Oliver's first dialling was not successful. She appeared to have connected herself to a Mrs Smith Potter, who seemed both annoyed and unhelpful and had no idea what the present telephone number might be of anyone who had lived in that particular flat before.

Mrs Oliver applied herself to an examination of the address book once more. She discovered two more addresses which were hastily scrawled over other numbers and did not seem wildly helpful. However, at the third attempt a somewhat illegible Ravenscroft seemed to emerge from the crossings out and initials and addresses.

A voice admitted to knowing Celia.

'Oh dear, yes. But she hasn't lived here for *years*. I think she was in Newcastle when I last heard from her.'

'Oh dear,' said Mrs Oliver, 'I'm afraid I haven't got that address.'

'No, I haven't got it either,' said the kindly girl. 'I think she went to be secretary to a veterinary surgeon.'

It did not sound very hopeful. Mrs Oliver tried once or twice more. The addresses in the latest of her two address books were no use, so she went back a bit further. She struck oil, as you might put it, when she came to the last one, which was for the year 1967.

'Oh, you mean Celia,' said a voice. 'Celia Ravenscroft, wasn't it? Or was it Finchwell?'

Mrs Oliver just prevented herself in time from saying, 'No, and it wasn't redbreast either.'

'A very competent girl,' said the voice. 'She worked for me for over a year and a half. Oh yes, very competent. I would have been quite happy if she had stayed longer. I think she went from here to somewhere in Harley Street, but I think I've got her address somewhere. Now let me see.' There was a long pause while Mrs X – name unknown – was seeing. 'I've got one address here. It seems to be in Islington somewhere. Do you think that's possible?'

Mrs Oliver said that anything was possible and thanked Mrs X very much and wrote it down.

'So difficult, isn't it, trying to find people's addresses. They do send them to you usually. You know, a sort of postcard or something of that kind. Personally I always seem to lose it.'

Mrs Oliver said that she herself also suffered in this respect. She tried the Islington number. A heavy, foreign voice replied to her.

'You want, yes – you tell me what? Yes, who live here?'

'Miss Celia Ravenscroft?'

'Oh yes, that is very true. Yes, yes she lives here. She

has a room on the second floor. She is out now and she not come home.'

'Will she be in later this evening?'

'Oh, she be home very soon now, I think, because she come home to dress for party and go out.'

Mrs Oliver thanked her for the information and rang off. 'Really,' said Mrs Oliver to herself, with some annoyance, 'girls!'

She tried to think how long it was since she had last seen her goddaughter, Celia. One lost touch. That was the whole point. Celia, she thought, was in London now. If her boy-friend was in London, or if the mother of her boy-friend was in London – all of it went together. Oh dear, thought Mrs Oliver, this really makes my head ache. 'Yes, Miss Livingstone?' she turned her head.

Miss Livingstone, looking rather unlike herself and decorated with a good many cobwebs and a general coating of dust, stood looking annoyed in the doorway holding a pile of dusty volumes.

'I don't know whether any of these things will be any use to you, Mrs Oliver. They seem to go back for a great many years.' She was disapproving.

'Bound to,' said Mrs Oliver.

'I don't know if there's anything particular you want me to search for.'

'I don't think so,' said Mrs Oliver, 'if you'll just put them on the corner of the sofa there I can look at them this evening.'

Miss Livingstone, looking more disapproving every moment, said, 'Very good, Mrs Oliver. I think I will just dust them first.'

'That will be very kind of you,' said Mrs Oliver, just stopping herself in time from saying – 'and for goodness' sake dust yourself as well. You've got six cobwebs in your left ear.'

She glanced at her watch and rang the Islington number again. The voice that answered this time was purely Anglo-Saxon and had a crisp sharpness about it that Mrs Oliver felt was rather satisfactory.

'Miss Ravenscroft? – Celia Ravenscroft?'

'Yes, this is Celia Ravenscroft.'

'Well, I don't expect you'll remember me very well. I'm Mrs Oliver. Ariadne Oliver. We haven't seen each other for a long time, but actually I'm your godmother.'

'Oh yes, of course. I know that. No, we haven't seen each other for a long time.'

'I wonder very much if I could see you, if you could come and see me, or whatever you like. Would you like to come to a meal or . . .'

'Well, it's rather difficult at present, where I'm working. I could come round this evening, if you like. About half past seven or eight. I've got a date later but . . .'

'If you do that I shall be very, very pleased,' said Mrs Oliver.

'Well, of course I will.'

'I'll give you the address.' Mrs Oliver gave it.

'Good. I'll be there. Yes, I know where that is, quite well.'

Mrs Oliver made a brief note on the telephone pad, and looked with some annoyance at Miss Livingstone, who had just come into the room struggling under the weight of a large album.

'I wondered if this could possibly be it, Mrs Oliver?'

'No, it couldn't,' said Mrs Oliver. 'That's got cookery recipes in it.'

'Oh dear,' said Miss Livingstone, 'so it has.'

'Well, I might as well look at some of them anyway,' said Mrs Oliver, removing the volume firmly. 'Go and have another look. You know, I've thought about the linen cupboard. Next door to the bathroom. You'd have to look on the top shelf above the bath towels. I do sometimes stick papers and books in there. Wait a minute. I'll come up and look myself.'

Ten minutes later Mrs Oliver was looking through the pages of a faded album. Miss Livingstone, having entered her final stage of martyrdom, was standing by the door. Unable to bear the sight of so much suffering, Mrs Oliver said,

'Well, that's all right. You might just take a look in the desk in the dining-room. The old desk. You know, the one that's broken a bit. See if you can find some more address books. Early ones. Anything up to about ten years old will be worth while having a look at. And after that,' said Mrs Oliver, 'I don't think I shall want anything more today.'

Miss Livingstone departed.

'I wonder,' said Mrs Oliver to herself, releasing a deep sigh as she sat down. She looked through the pages of the birthday book. 'Who's better pleased? She to go or I to see her go? After Celia has come and gone, I shall have to have a busy evening.'

Taking a new exercise book from the pile she kept on a small table by her desk, she entered various dates, possible addresses and names, looked up one or two more things in the telephone book and then proceeded to ring up Monsieur Hercule Poirot.

'Ah, is that you, Monsieur Poirot?'

'Yes, madame, it is I myself.'

'Have you done anything?' said Mrs Oliver.

'I beg your pardon – have I done what?'

'Anything,' said Mrs Oliver. 'What I asked you about yesterday.'

'Yes, certainly. I have put things in motion. I have arranged to make certain enquiries.'

'But you haven't made them yet,' said Mrs Oliver, who had a poor view of what the male view was of doing something.

'And you, *chère madame*?'

'I have been very busy,' said Mrs Oliver.

'Ah! And what have you been doing, madame?'

'Assembling elephants,' said Mrs Oliver, 'if that means anything to you.'

'I think I can understand what you mean, yes.'

'It's not very easy, looking into the past,' said Mrs Oliver. 'It is astonishing, really, how many people one does remember when one comes to look up names. My word, the silly things they write in birthday books sometimes, too. I can't think why when I was about sixteen or seventeen or even thirty, I wanted people to write in my birthday book. There's a sort of quotation from a poet for every particular day in the year. Some of them are terribly silly.'

'You are encouraged in your search?'

'Not quite encouraged,' said Mrs Oliver. 'But I still think I'm on the right lines. I've rung up my goddaughter – '

'Ah. And you are going to see her?'

'Yes, she is coming to see me. Tonight between seven and eight, if she doesn't run out on me. One never knows. Young people are very unreliable.'

'She appeared pleased that you had rung her up?'

'I don't know,' said Mrs Oliver, 'not particularly pleased. She's got a very incisive voice and – I remember now, the last time I saw her, that must be about six years ago, I thought then that she was rather frightening.'

'Frightening? In what way?'

'What I mean is that she was more likely to bully me than I would be to bully her.'

'That may be a good thing and not a bad thing.'

'Oh, do you think so?'

'If people have made up their minds that they do not wish to like you, that they are quite sure they do not like you, they will get more pleasure out of making you aware of the fact and in that way will release more information to you than they would have done if they were trying to be amiable and agreeable.'

'Sucking up to me, you mean? Yes, you have something there. You mean then they tell you things that they thought would please you. And the other way they'd be annoyed with you and they'd say things that they'd hope would annoy you. I wonder if Celia's like that? I really remember her much better when she was five years old than at any other age. She had a nursery governess and she used to throw her boots at her.'

'The governess at the child, or the child at the governess?'

'The child at the governess, of course!' said Mrs Oliver.

She replaced the receiver and went over to the sofa to examine the various piled-up memories of the past. She murmured names under her breath.

'Mariana Josephine Pontarlier – of course, yes, I haven't thought of her for years – I thought she was dead. Anna Braceby – yes, yes, she lived in that part of the world – I wonder now – '

Continuing all this, time passed – she was quite surprised when the bell rang. She went out herself to open the door.

Chapter 4

CELIA

A tall girl was standing on the mat outside. Just for a moment Mrs Oliver was startled looking at her. So this was Celia. The impression of vitality and of life was really very strong. Mrs Oliver had the feeling which one does not often get.

Here, she thought, was someone who *meant* something.

Aggressive, perhaps, could be difficult, could be almost dangerous perhaps. One of those girls who had a mission in life, who was dedicated to violence, perhaps, who went in for causes. But interesting. Definitely interesting.

'Come in, Celia,' she said. 'It's such a long time since I saw you. The last time, as far as I remember, was at a wedding. You were a bridesmaid. You wore apricot chiffon, I remember, and large bunches of – I can't remember what it was, something that looked like Golden Rod.'

'Probably *was* Golden Rod,' said Celia Ravenscroft. 'We sneezed a lot – with hay fever. It was a terrible wedding. I know. Martha Leghorn, wasn't it? Ugliest bridesmaids' dresses I've ever seen. Certainly the ugliest I've ever worn!'

'Yes. They weren't very becoming to anybody. You looked better than most, if I may say so.'

'Well, it's nice of you to say that,' said Celia. 'I didn't feel my best.'

Mrs Oliver indicated a chair and manipulated a couple of decanters.

'Like sherry or something else?'

'No. I'd like sherry.'

'There you are, then. I suppose it seems rather odd to you,' said Mrs Oliver. 'My ringing you up suddenly like this.'

'Oh no, I don't know that it does particularly.'

'I'm not a very conscientious godmother, I'm afraid.'

'Why should you be, at my age?'

'You're right there,' said Mrs Oliver. 'One's duties, one feels, end at a certain time. Not that I ever really fulfilled mine. I don't remember coming to your Confirmation.'

'I believe the duty of a godmother is to make you learn your catechism and a few things like that, isn't it? Renounce the devil and all his works in my name,' said Celia. A faint, humorous smile came to her lips.

She was being very amiable but all the same, thought Mrs Oliver, she's rather a dangerous girl in some ways.

'Well, I'll tell you why I've been trying to get hold of you,' said Mrs Oliver. 'The whole thing is rather peculiar. I don't often go out to literary parties, but as it happened I did go out to one the day before yesterday.'

'Yes, I know,' said Celia. 'I saw mention of it in the paper, and you had your name in it, too, Mrs Ariadne Oliver, and I rather wondered because I know you don't usually go to that sort of thing.'

'No,' said Mrs Oliver. 'I rather wish I hadn't gone to that one.'

'Didn't you enjoy it?'

'Yes, I did in a way because I hadn't been to one before. And so – well, the first time there's always something that amuses you. But,' she added, 'there's usually something that annoys you as well.'

'And something happened to annoy you?'

'Yes. And it's connected in an odd sort of way with you. And I thought – well, I thought I ought to tell you about it because I didn't like what happened. I didn't like it at all.'

'Sounds intriguing,' said Celia, and sipped her sherry.

'There was a woman there who came and spoke to me. I didn't know her and she didn't know me.'

'Still, I suppose that often happens to you,' said Celia.

'Yes, invariably,' said Mrs Oliver. 'It's one of the – hazards of literary life. People come up to you and say "I do love your books so much and I'm so pleased to be able to meet you." That sort of thing.'

'I was secretary to a writer once. I do know about that sort of thing and how difficult it is.'

'Yes, well, there was some of that too, but that I was prepared for. And then this woman came up to me and she said "I believe you have a goddaughter called Celia Ravenscroft." '

'Well, that was a bit odd,' said Celia. 'Just coming up to you and saying that. It seems to me she ought to have led into it more gradually. You know, talking about your books first and how much she'd enjoyed the last one, or something like that. And then sliding into me. What had she got against me?'

'As far as I know she hadn't got anything against you,' said Mrs Oliver.

'Was she a friend of mine?'

'I don't know,' said Mrs Oliver.

There was a silence. Celia sipped some more sherry and looked very searchingly at Mrs Oliver.

'You know,' she said, 'you're rather intriguing me. I can't see quite what you're leading into.'

'Well,' said Mrs Oliver, 'I hope you won't be angry with me.'

'Why should I be angry with you?'

'Well, because I'm going to tell you something, or repeat something, and you might say it's no business of mine or I ought to keep quiet about it and not mention it.'

'You've aroused my curiosity,' said Celia.

'Her name she mentioned to me. She was a Mrs Burton-Cox.'

'Oh!' Celia's 'Oh' was rather distinctive. 'Oh.'

'You know her?'

'Yes, I know her,' said Celia.

'Well, I thought you must because –'

'Because of what?'

'Because of something she said.'

'What – about me? That she knew me?'

'She said that she thought her son might be going to marry you.'

Celia's expression changed. Her eyebrows went up, came down again. She looked very hard at Mrs Oliver.

'You want to know if that's so or not?'

'No,' said Mrs Oliver, 'I don't particularly want to know. I merely mention that because it's one of the first things she said to me. She said because you were my goddaughter, I might be able to ask you to give me some information. I presume that she meant that if the information was given to me I was to pass it on to her.'

'What information?'

'Well, I don't suppose you'll like what I'm going to say now,' said Mrs Oliver. 'I didn't like it myself. In fact, it gives me a very nasty feeling all down my spine because I think it was – well, such awful cheek. Awful bad manners. Absolutely unpardonable. She said, "Can you find out if her father murdered her mother or if her mother murdered her father." '

'She said that to you? Asked you to do *that*?'

'Yes.'

'And she didn't know you? I mean, apart from being an authoress and being at the party?'

'She didn't know me at all. She'd never met me, I'd never met her.'

'Didn't you find that extraordinary?'

'I don't know that I'd find anything extraordinary that that woman said. She struck me,' said Mrs Oliver, 'if I may say so, as a particularly odious woman.'

'Oh yes. She is a particularly odious woman.'

'And are you going to marry her son?'

'Well, we've considered the question. I don't know. You knew what she was talking about?'

'Well, I know what I suppose anyone would know who

41

was acquainted with your family.'

'That my father and mother, after he had retired from the Army, bought a house in the country, that they went out one day for a walk together, a walk along the cliff path. That they were found there, both of them shot. There was a revolver lying there. It belonged to my father. He had had two revolvers in the house, it seems. There was nothing to say whether it was a suicide pact or whether my father killed my mother and then shot himself, or my mother shot my father and then killed herself. But perhaps you know all this already.'

'I know it after a fashion,' said Mrs Oliver. 'It happened I think about twelve years ago.'

'About that, yes.'

'And you were about twelve or fourteen at the time.'

'Yes . . .'

'I don't know much about it,' said Mrs Oliver. 'I wasn't even in England myself. At the time – I was on a lecture tour in America. I simply read it in the paper. It was given a lot of space in the press because it was difficult to know the real facts – there did not seem to be any motive. Your father and mother had always been happy together and lived on good terms. I remember that being mentioned. I was interested because I had known your father and mother when we were all much younger, especially your mother. I was at school with her. After that our ways led apart. I married and went somewhere and she married and went out, as far as I remember, to Malaya or some place like that, with her soldier husband. But she did ask me to be godmother to one of her children. You. Since your mother and father were living abroad, I saw very little of them for many years. I saw you occasionally.'

'Yes. You used to take me out from school. I remember that. Gave me some specially good feeds, too. Lovely food you gave me.'

'You were an unusual child. You liked caviar.'

'I still do,' said Celia, 'though I don't get it offered to me very often.'

'I was shocked to read this mention of things in the paper. Very little was said. I gathered it was a kind of open verdict. No particular motive. Nothing to show. No accounts of quarrel, there was no suggestion of there having been an attack from outside. I was shocked by it,' said Mrs Oliver, 'and then I forgot it. I wondered once or twice what could have led to it, but as I was not in the country – I was doing a tour at the time, in America as I've said – the whole thing passed out of my mind. It was some years later when I next saw you and naturally I did not speak of it to you.'

'No,' said Celia, 'I appreciate that.'

'All through life,' Mrs Oliver said, 'one comes across very curious things that happen to friends or to acquaintances. With friends, of course, very often you have some idea of what led to – whatever the incident might be. But if it's a long time since you've heard them discussed or talked to them, you are quite in the dark and there is nobody that you can show too much curiosity to about the occasion.'

'You were always very nice to me,' said Celia. 'You sent me nice presents, a particularly nice present when I was twenty-one, I remember.'

'That's the time when girls need some extra cash in hand,' said Mrs Oliver, 'because there are so many things they want to do and have just then.'

'Yes, I always thought you were an understanding person and not – well, you know what some people are like. Always questioning, and asking things and wanting to know all about you. You never asked questions. You used to take me out to shows, or give me nice meals, and talk to me as though, well, as though everything was all right and you were just a distant relation of the family. I've appreciated that. I've known so many nosey-parkers in my life.'

'Yes. Everyone comes up against that sooner or later,' said Mrs Oliver. 'But you see now what upset me at this particular party. It seems an extraordinary thing to be asked to do by a complete stranger like Mrs Burton-Cox. I couldn't imagine why she should want to know. It was no business of hers, surely. Unless – '

'You thought it was, unless it was something to do with my marrying Desmond. Desmond is her son.'

'Yes, I suppose it could have been, but I couldn't see how, or what business it was of hers.'

'Everything's her business. She's nosey – in fact she's what you said she was, an odious woman.'

'But I gather Desmond isn't odious.'

'No. No, I'm very fond of Desmond and Desmond is fond of me. I don't like his mother.'

'Does he like his mother?'

'I don't really know,' said Celia. 'I suppose he might like her – anything's possible, isn't it? Anyway, I don't want to get married at present, I don't feel like it. And there are a lot of – oh, well, difficulties, you know, there are a lot of fors and againsts. It must have made you feel rather curious,' said Celia. 'I mean, why Mrs Nosey Cox should have asked you to try and worm things out of me and then run along and spill it all to her – Are you asking me that particular question by the way?'

'You mean, am I asking you whether you think or know that your mother killed your father or your father killed your mother, or whether it was a double suicide. Is that what you mean?'

'Well, I suppose it is, in a way. But I think I have to ask you also, *if* you were wanting to ask me that, whether you were doing so with the idea of giving Mrs Burton-Cox the information you obtained, in case you did receive any information from me.'

'No,' said Mrs Oliver. 'Quite decidedly no. I shouldn't dream of telling the odious woman anything of the sort. I shall tell her quite firmly that it is not any business of hers or of mine, and that I have no intention of obtaining information from you and retailing it to her.'

'Well, that's what I thought,' said Celia. 'I thought I could trust you to that extent. I don't mind telling you what I do know. Such as it is.'

'You needn't. I'm not asking you for it.'

'No. I can quite see that. But I'll give you the answer all the same. The answer is – nothing.'

'Nothing,' said Mrs Oliver thoughtfully.

'No. I wasn't there at the time. I mean, I wasn't in the house at the time. I can't remember now quite where I was. I think I was at school in Switzerland, or else I was staying with a school friend during the school holidays. You see, it's all rather mixed up in my mind by now.'

'I suppose,' said Mrs Oliver doubtfully, 'it wouldn't be likely that you *would* know. Considering your age at the time.'

'I'd be interested,' said Celia, 'to know just what you feel about that. Do you think it would be likely for me to know all about it? Or not to know?'

'Well, you said you weren't in the house. If you'd been in the house at the time, then yes, I think it would be quite likely that you might know something. Children do. Teenagers do. People of that age know a lot, they see a lot, they don't talk about it very often. But they do know things that the outside world wouldn't know, and they do know things that they wouldn't be willing, shall we say, to tell to police enquirers.'

'No. You're being quite sensible. I wouldn't've known. I don't think I did know. I don't think I had any idea. What did the police think? You don't mind my asking you that, I hope, because I should be interested. You see, I never read any account of the inquest or anything like that or the enquiry into it.'

'I think they thought it was a double suicide, but I don't think they ever had any inkling as to the reason for it.'

'Do you want to know what I think?'

'Not if you don't want me to know,' said Mrs Oliver.

'But I expect you are interested. After all, you write crime stories about people who kill themselves or kill each other, or who have reasons for things. I should think you would be interested.'

'Yes, I'll admit that,' said Mrs Oliver. 'But the last thing I want to do is to offend you by seeking for information which is no business of mine to know.'

'Well, I wondered,' said Celia. 'I've often wondered from time to time why, and how, but I knew very little about things. I mean, about how things were going on at home. The holidays before that I had been away on exchange on the Continent, so I hadn't seen my mother and father really very recently. I mean, they'd come out to Switzerland and taken me out from school once or twice, but that was all. They seemed much as usual, but they seemed older. My father, I think, was ailing. I mean, getting feebler. I don't know if it was heart or what it was. One doesn't really think about that. My mother, too, she was going rather nervy. Not hypochondriac but a little inclined to fuss over her health. They were on good terms, quite friendly. There wasn't anything that I noticed. Only sometimes one would, well, sometimes one gets ideas. One doesn't think they're true or necessarily right at all, but one just wonders if – '

'I don't think we'd better talk about it any more,' said Mrs Oliver. 'We don't need to know or find out. The whole thing's over and done with. The verdict was quite satisfactory. No means to show, or motive, or anything like that. But there was no question of your father having deliberately killed your mother, or of your mother having deliberately killed your father.'

'If I thought which was most likely,' said Celia, 'I would

45

think my father killed my mother. Because, you see, it's more natural for a man to shoot anyone, I think. To shoot a woman for whatever reason it was. I don't think a woman, or a woman like my mother, would be so likely to shoot my father. If she wanted him dead, I should think she might have chosen some other method. But I don't think either of them wanted the other one dead.'

'So it could have been an outsider.'

'Yes, but what does one mean by an outsider?' said Celia. 'Who else was there living in the house?'

'A housekeeper, elderly, rather blind and rather deaf, a foreign girl, an au pair girl, she'd been my governess once – she was awfully nice – she came back to look after my mother who had been in hospital – And there was an aunt whom I never loved much. I don't think any of them could have been likely to have any grudge against my parents. There was nobody who profited by their deaths, except, I suppose, myself and my brother Edward, who was four years younger than I was. We inherited what money there was but it wasn't very much. My father had his pension, of course. My mother had a small income of her own. No. There was nothing there of any importance.'

'I'm sorry,' said Mrs Oliver. 'I'm sorry if I've distressed you by asking all this.'

'You haven't distressed me. You've brought it up in my mind a little and it has interested me. Because, you see, I am of an age now that I wish I did know. I knew and was fond of them, as one is fond of parents. Not passionately, just normally, but I realize I don't know what they were really *like*. What their life was like. What *mattered* to them. I don't know anything about it at all. I wish I did know. It's like a burr, something sticking into you, and you can't leave it alone. Yes. I would like to *know*. Because then, you see, I shouldn't have to think about it any more.'

'So you do? Think about it?'

Celia looked at her for a moment. She seemed to be trying to come to a decision.

'Yes,' she said, 'I think about it nearly all the time. I'm getting to have a thing about it, if you know what I mean. And Desmond feels the same.'

Chapter 5

OLD SINS HAVE LONG SHADOWS

Hercule Poirot let the revolving door wind him round. Arresting the swing of it with one hand, he stepped forward into the small restaurant. There were not many people there. It was an unfashionable time of day, but his eyes soon saw the man he had come to meet. The square, solid bulk of Superintendent Spence rose from the table in one corner.

'Good,' he said. 'You have arrived here. You had no difficulty in finding it?'

'None at all. Your instructions were most adequate.'

'Let me introduce you now. This is Chief Superintendent Garroway. Monsieur Hercule Poirot.'

Garroway was a tall, thin man with a lean, ascetic face, grey hair which left a small round spot like a tonsure, so that he had a faint resemblance to an ecclesiastic.

'This is wonderful,' said Poirot.

'I am retired now, of course,' said Garroway, 'but one remembers. Yes, certain things one remembers, although they are past and gone, and the general public probably remembers nothing about them. But yes.'

Hercule Poirot very nearly said 'Elephants do remember,' but checked himself in time. That phrase was so associated in his mind now with Mrs Ariadne Oliver that he found it difficult to restrain it from his tongue in many clearly unsuitable categories.

'I hope you have not been getting impatient,' said Superintendent Spence.

He pulled forward a chair, and the three men sat down. A menu was brought. Superintendent Spence, who was clearly addicted to this particular restaurant, offered tentative words of advice. Garroway and Poirot made their choice. Then, leaning back a little in their chairs and sipping glasses of sherry, they contemplated each other for some minutes in silence before speaking.

'I must apologize to you,' said Poirot, 'I really must apologize to you for coming to you with my demands about an affair which is over and done with.'

'What interests me,' said Spence, 'is what has interested you. I thought first that it was unlike you to have this wish to delve in the past. It is connected with something that has occurred nowadays, or is it sudden curiosity about a rather inexplicable, perhaps, case? Do you agree with that?'

He looked across the table.

'Inspector Garroway,' he said, 'as he was at that time, was the officer in charge of the investigations into the Ravenscroft shooting. He was an old friend of mine and so I had no difficulty in getting in touch with him.'

'And he was kind enough to come here today,' said Poirot, 'simply because I must admit to a curiosity which I am sure I have no right to feel about an affair that is past and done with.'

'Well, I wouldn't say that,' said Garroway. 'We all have interests in certain cases that are past. Did Lizzie Borden really kill her father and mother with an axe? There are people who still do not think so. Who killed Charles Bravo and why? There are several different ideas, mostly not very well founded. But still people try to find alternative explanations.'

His keen, shrewd eyes looked across at Poirot.

'And Monsieur Poirot, if I am not mistaken, has occasionally shown a leaning towards looking into cases, going back, shall we say, for murder, back into the past, twice, perhaps three times.'

'Three times, certainly,' said Superintendent Spence.

'Once, I think I am right, by request of a Canadian girl.'

'That is so,' said Poirot. 'A Canadian girl, very vehement, very passionate, very forceful, who had come here to investigate a murder for which her mother had been condemned to death, although she died before sentence was carried out. Her daughter was convinced that her mother had been innocent.'

'And you agreed?' said Garroway.

'I did not agree,' said Poirot, 'when she first told me of the matter. But she was very vehement and very sure.'

'It was natural for a daughter to wish her mother to have been innocent and to try and prove against all appearances that she was innocent,' said Spence.

'It was just a little more than that,' said Poirot. 'She convinced me of the type of woman her mother was.'

'A woman incapable of murder?'

'No,' said Poirot, 'it would be very difficult, and I am sure both of you agree with me, to think there is anyone quite incapable of murder if one knows what kind of person they are, what led up to it. But in that particular case, the mother never protested her innocence. She appeared to be quite content to be sentenced. That was curious to begin with. Was she a defeatist? It did not seem so. When I began to enquire, it became clear that she was not a defeatist. She was, one would say, almost the opposite of it.'

Garroway looked interested. He leaned across the table, twisting a bit of bread off the roll on his plate.

'And was she innocent?'

'Yes,' said Poirot. 'She was innocent.'

'And that surprised you?'

'Not by the time I realized it,' said Poirot. 'There were one or two things – one thing in particular – that showed she *could not* have been guilty. One fact that nobody had appreciated at the time. Knowing that one had only to look at what there was, shall we say, on the menu in the way of looking elsewhere.'*

Grilled trout was put in front of them at this point.

'There was another case, too, where you looked into the past, not quite in the same way,' continued Spence. 'A girl who said at a party that she had once seen a murder committed.'†

'There again one had to – how shall I put it? – step backwards instead of forward,' said Poirot. 'Yes, that is very true.'

'And had the girl seen the murder committed?'

'No,' said Poirot, 'because it was the wrong girl. This trout is delicious,' he added, with appreciation.

'They do all fish dishes very well here,' said Superintendent Spence.

He helped himself from the sauce boat proffered to him.

'A most delicious sauce,' he added.

Silent appreciation of food filled the next three minutes.

'When Spence came along to me,' said Superintendent Garroway, 'asking if I remembered anything about the Ravenscroft case, I was intrigued and delighted at once.'

'You haven't forgotten all about it?'

'Not the Ravenscroft case. It wasn't an easy case to forget about.'

* *Five Little Pigs*
† *Hallowe'en Party*

'You agree,' said Poirot, 'that there were discrepancies about it? Lack of proof, alternative solutions?'

'No,' said Garroway, 'nothing of that kind. All the evidence recorded the visible facts. Deaths of which there were several former examples, yes, all plain sailing. And yet – '

'Well?' said Poirot.

'And yet it was all wrong,' said Garroway.

'Ah,' said Spence. He looked interested.

'That's what you felt once, isn't it?' said Poirot, turning to him.

'In the case of Mrs McGinty. Yes.'*

'You weren't satisfied,' said Poirot, 'when that extremely difficult young man was arrested. He had every reason for doing it, he looked as though he had done it, everyone thought he had done it. But you knew he hadn't done it. You were so sure of it that you came to me and told me to go along to see what I could find out.'

'See if you could help – and you did help, didn't you?' said Spence.

Poirot sighed.

'Fortunately, yes. But what a tiresome young man he was. If ever a young man deserved to be hanged, not because he had done a murder but because he wouldn't help anyone to prove that he hadn't. Now we have the Ravenscroft case. You say, Superintendent Garroway, something was wrong?'

'Yes, I felt quite sure of it if you understand what I mean.'

'I do understand,' said Poirot. 'And so does Spence. One does come across these things sometimes. The proofs are there, the motive, the opportunity, the clues, the *mise-en-scène,* it's all there. A complete blueprint, as you might say. But all the same, those whose profession it is, *know.* They know that it's all wrong, just like a critic in the artistic world knows when a picture is all wrong. Knows when it's a fake and not the real thing.'

'There wasn't anything I could do about it, either,' said Superintendent Garroway. 'I looked into it, around it, up above it and down below it, as you might say. I talked to the people. There was nothing there. It looked like a suicide pact, it had all the marks of the suicide pact. Alternatively, of course, it could be a husband who shot a wife and then himself, or a wife who shot her husband and then herself. All those three things happen. When one comes across them, one knows they have happened. But in most cases one has

* *Mrs McGinty's Dead.*

some idea of *why*.'

'There wasn't any real idea of *why* in this case, was that it?' said Poirot.

'Yes. That's it. You see, the moment you begin to enquire into a case, to enquire about people and things, you get a very good picture as a rule of what their lives have been like. This was a couple, ageing, the husband with a good record, a wife affectionate, pleasant, on good terms together. That's a thing one soon finds out about. They were happy living together. They went for walks, they played picquet, and poker patience with each other in the evenings, they had children who caused them no particular anxiety. A boy in school in England and a girl in a *pensionnat* in Switzerland. There was nothing wrong with their lives as far as one could tell. From such medical evidence as one could obtain, there was nothing definitely wrong with their health. The husband had suffered from high blood pressure at one time, but was in good condition by the taking of suitable medicaments which kept him on an even keel. His wife was slightly deaf and had had a little minor heart trouble, nothing to be worried about. Of course it could be, as does happen sometimes, that one or other of them had fears for their health. There are a lot of people who are in good health but are quite convinced they have cancer, are quite sure that they won't live another year. Sometimes that leads to their taking their own life. The Ravenscrofts didn't seem that kind of person. They seemed well balanced and placid.'

'So what did you really think?' said Poirot.

'The trouble is that I couldn't think. Looking back, I say to myself it was suicide. It could only have been suicide. For some reason or other they decided that life was unbearable to them. Not through financial trouble, not through health difficulties, not because of unhappiness. And there, you see, I came to a full stop. It had all the marks of suicide. I cannot see any other thing that could have happened except suicide. They went for a walk. In that walk they took a revolver with them. The revolver lay between the two bodies. There were blurred fingerprints of both of them. Both of them in fact had handled it, but there was nothing to show who had fired it last. One tends to think the husband perhaps shot his wife and then himself. That is only because it seems more likely. Well, why? A great many years have passed. When something reminds me now and again, something I read in the papers of bodies, a husband's and wife's bodies somewhere, lying dead, having taken their own lives apparently, I think back and then I wonder again what happened in the Ravenscroft case. Twelve years ago or fourteen and I still remember the Ravenscroft case and wonder – well, just the one word, I think. Why – why – why? Did the husband really hate his wife, and had hated her for a long time? Did the wife really hate her husband and want to get rid of him? Did they go on hating each other until they could bear it no longer?'

Garroway broke off another piece of bread and chewed at it.

'You got some idea, Monsieur Poirot? Has somebody come to you and told you something that has awakened your interest particularly? Do you know something that might explain the "Why"?'

'No. All the same,' said Poirot, 'you must have had a theory. Come now, you had a theory?'

'You're quite right, of course. One does have theories. One expects them all, or one of them at least, to work out, but they don't usually. I think that my theory was in the end that you couldn't look for the cause, because one didn't know enough. What *did* I know about them? General Ravenscroft was close on sixty, his wife was thirty-five. All I knew of them, strictly speaking, was the last five or six years of their lives. The General had retired on a pension. They had come back to England from abroad and all the evidence that came to me, all the knowledge, was of a brief period during which they had first a house at Bournemouth and then moved to where they lived in the home where the tragedy took place. They had lived there peacefully, happily, their children came home there for school holidays. It was a peaceful period, I should say, at the end of what one presumed was a peaceful life. But then I thought, but how much did I know of that peaceful life? I knew of their life after retirement in England, of their family. There was no financial motive, no motive of hatred, no motive of sexual involvement, of intrusive love-affairs. No. But there *was* a period before that. What did I know about that? What I knew was a life spent mostly abroad with occasional visits home, a good record for the man, pleasant remembrances of her from friends of the wife's. There was no outstanding tragedy, dispute, nothing that one knew of. But then I mightn't have known. One doesn't know. There was a period of, say, twenty-thirty years, years from childhood to the time they married, the time they lived abroad in Malaya and other places. Perhaps the root of the tragedy was there. There is a proverb my grandmother used to repeat: *Old sins have long shadows.* Was the cause of death some long shadow, a shadow from the past? That's not an easy thing to find out about. You find out about a man's record, what friends or acquaintances say, but you don't know any inner details. Well, I think little by little the theory grew up in my mind that that would have been the place to look, if I could have looked. Something that had happened then, in another country, perhaps. Something that had been thought to be forgotten, to have passed out of existence, but which still perhaps existed. A grudge from the past, some happening that nobody knew about, that had happened elsewhere, not in their life in England, but which may have been there. If one had known where to look for it.'

'Not the sort of thing, you mean,' said Poirot, 'that anybody would remember. I mean, remember nowadays. Something that no friends of theirs in England, perhaps, would have known about.'

'Their friends in England seem to have been mostly made since retirement, though I suppose old friends did come and visit them or see them occasionally. But one doesn't hear about things that happened in the past. People forget.'

'Yes,' said Poirot, thoughtfully. 'People forget.'

'They're not like elephants,' said Superintendent Garroway, giving a faint smile. 'Elephants, they always say, remember everything.'

'It is odd that you should say that,' said Poirot.

'That I should say that about long sins?'

'Not so much that. It was your mention of elephants that interested me.'

Superintendent Garroway looked at Poirot with some surprise. He seemed to be waiting for more. Spence also cast a quick glance at his old friend.

'Something that happened out East, perhaps,' he suggested. 'I mean – well, that's where elephants come from, isn't it? Or from Africa. Anyway, who's been talking to you about elephants?' he added.

'A friend of mine happened to mention them,' said Poirot. 'Someone *you* know,' he said to Superintendent Spence. 'Mrs Oliver.'

'Oh, Mrs Ariadne Oliver. Well!' He paused.

'Well what?' said Poirot.

'Well, does she know something, then?' he asked.

'I do not think so as yet,' said Poirot, 'but she might know something before very long.' He added thoughtfully, 'She's that kind of person. She gets around, if you know what I mean.'

'Yes,' said Spence. 'Yes. Has she got any ideas?' he asked.

'Do you mean Mrs Ariadne Oliver, the writer?' asked Garroway with some interest.

'That's the one,' said Spence.

'Does she know a good deal about crime? I know she writes crime stories. I've never known where she got her ideas from or her facts.'

'Her ideas,' said Poirot, 'come out of her head. Her facts — well, that's more difficult.' He paused for a moment.

'What are you thinking of, Poirot, something in particular?'

'Yes,' said Poirot. 'I ruined one of her stories once, or so she tells me. She had just had a very good idea about a fact, something that had to do with a long-sleeved woollen vest. I asked her something over the telephone and it put the idea for the story out of her head. She reproaches me at intervals.'

'Dear, dear,' said Spence. 'Sounds rather like that parsley that sank into the butter on a hot day. You know. Sherlock Holmes and the dog who did nothing in the night time.'

'Did they have a dog?' asked Poirot.

'I beg your pardon?'

'I said did they have a dog? General and Lady Ravenscroft. Did they take a dog for that walk with them on the day they were shot? The Ravenscrofts.'

'They had a dog — yes,' said Garroway. 'I suppose, I suppose they did take him for a walk most days.'

'If it had been one of Mrs Oliver's stories,' said Spence, 'you ought to have found the dog howling over the two dead bodies. But that didn't happen.'

Garroway shook his head.

'I wonder where the dog is now?' said Poirot.

'Buried in somebody's garden, I expect,' said Garroway. 'It's fourteen years ago.'

'So we can't go and ask the dog, can we?' said Poirot. He added thoughtfully, 'A pity. It's astonishing, you know, what dogs can know. Who was there exactly in the house? I mean on the day when the crime happened?'

'I brought you a list,' said Superintendent Garroway, 'in case you like to consult it. Mrs Whittaker, the elderly cook-housekeeper. It was her day out so we couldn't get much from her that was helpful. A visitor was staying there who had been governess to the Ravenscroft children once, I believe. Mrs Whittaker was rather deaf and slightly blind. She couldn't tell us anything of interest, except that recently Lady Ravenscroft had been in hospital or in a nursing home – for nerves but not illness, apparently. There was a gardener, too.'

'But a stranger might have come from outside. A stranger from the past. That's your idea, Superintendent Garroway?'

'Not so much an idea as just a theory.'

Poirot was silent, he was thinking of a time when he had asked to go back into the past, had studied five people out of the past who had reminded him of the nursery rhyme 'Five little pigs.' Interesting it had been, and in the end rewarding, because he had found out the truth.

Chapter 6

AN OLD FRIEND REMEMBERS

When Mrs Oliver returned to the house the following morning, she found Miss Livingstone waiting for her.

'There have been two telephone calls, Mrs Oliver.'

'Yes?' said Mrs Oliver.

'The first one was from Crichton and Smith. They wanted to know whether you had chosen the lime-green brocade or the pale blue one.'

'I haven't made up my mind yet,' said Mrs Oliver. 'Just remind me tomorrow morning, will you? I'd like to see it by night light.'

'And the other was from a foreigner, a Mr Hercule Poirot, I believe.'

'Oh, yes,' said Mrs Oliver. 'What did he want?'

'He asked if you would be able to call and see him this afternoon.'

'That will be quite impossible,' said Mrs Oliver. 'Ring him up, will you? I've got to go out again at once, as a matter of fact. Did he leave a telephone number?'

'Yes, he did.'

'That's all right, then. We won't have to look it up again.

All right. Just ring him. Tell him I'm sorry that I can't but that I'm out on the track of an elephant.'

'I beg your pardon?' said Miss Livingston.

'Say that I'm on the track of an elephant.'

'Oh yes,' said Miss Livingstone, looking shrewdly at her employer to see if she was right in the feelings that she sometimes had that Mrs Ariadne Oliver, though a successful novelist, was at the same time not quite right in the head.

'I've never hunted elephants before,' said Mrs Oliver. 'It's quite an interesting thing to do, though.'

She went into the sitting-room, opened the top volume of the assorted books on the sofa, most of them looking rather the worse for wear, since she had toiled through them the evening before and written out a paper with various addresses.

'Well, one has got to make a start somewhere,' she said. 'On the whole I think that if Julia hasn't gone completely off her rocker by now, I might start with her. She always had ideas and after all, she knew that part of the country because she lived near there. Yes, I think we'll start with Julia.'

'There are four letters here for you to sign,' said Miss Livingstone.

'I can't be bothered now,' said Mrs Oliver. 'I really can't spare a moment. I've got to go down to Hampton Court, and it's quite a long ride.'

The Honourable Julia Carstairs, struggling with some slight difficulty out of her armchair, the difficulty that those over the age of seventy have when rising to their feet after prolonged rest, even a possible nap, stepped forward, peering a little to see who it was who had just been announced by the faithful retainer who shared the apartment which she occupied in her status of a member of 'Homes for the Privileged'. Being slightly deaf, the name had not come clearly to her. Mrs Gulliver. Was that it? But she didn't remember a Mrs Gulliver. She advanced on slightly shaky knees, still peering forward.

'I don't expect you'll remember me, it's so many years since we met.'

Like many elderly people, Mrs Carstairs could remember voices better than she did faces.

'Why,' she exclaimed, 'it's – dear me, it's Ariadne! My dear, how very nice to see you.'

Greetings passed.

'I just happened to be in this part of the world,' explained Mrs Oliver. 'I had to come down to see someone not far from here. And then I remembered that looking in my address book last night I had seen that this was quite near where you had your apartment. Delightful, isn't it?' she added, looking round.

'Not too bad,' said Mrs Carstairs. 'Not quite all it's written up to be, you know. But it has many advantages. One brings one's own furniture and things like that, and there is a central restaurant where you can have a meal, or you can have your own things, of course. Oh yes, it's very good, really. The grounds are charming and well kept up. But sit down, Ariadne, do sit down. You look very well. I saw you were at a literary lunch the other day, in the paper. How odd it is that one just sees something in the paper and almost the next day one meets the person. Quite extraordinary.'

'I know,' said Mrs Oliver, taking the chair that was offered her. 'Things do go like that, don't they.'

'You are still living in London?'

Mrs Oliver said yes, she was still living in London. She then entered into what she thought of in her own mind, with vague memories of going to dancing class as a child, as the first figure of the Lancers. Advance, retreat, hands out, turn round twice, whirl round, and so on.

She enquired after Mrs Carstairs's daughter and about the two grandchildren, and she asked about the other daughter, what she was doing. She appeared to be doing it in New Zealand. Mrs Carstairs did not seem to be quite sure what it was. Some kind of social research. Mrs Carstairs pressed an electric bell that rested on the arm of her chair, and ordered Emma to bring tea. Mrs Oliver begged her not to bother. Julia Carstairs said:

'Of course Ariadne has got to have tea.'

The two ladies leant back. The second and third figures of the Lancers. Old friends. Other people's children. The death of friends.

'It must be years since I saw you last,' said Mrs Carstairs.

'I think it was at the Llewellyns' wedding,' said Mrs Oliver.

'Yes, that must have been about it. How terrible Moira looked as a bridesmaid. That dreadfully unbecoming shade of apricot they wore.'

'I know. It didn't suit them.'

'I don't think weddings are nearly as pretty as they used

to be in our day. Some of them seem to wear such very peculiar clothes. The other day one of my friends went to a wedding and she said the bridegroom was dressed in some sort of quilted white satin and ruffles at his neck. Made of Valenciennes lace, I believe. *Most* peculiar. And the girl was wearing a very peculiar trouser suit. Also white but it was stamped with green shamrocks all over.'

'Well, my dear Ariadne, can you imagine it. Really, extraordinary. In church too. If I'd been a clergyman I'd have refused to marry them.'

Tea came. Talk continued.

'I saw my goddaughter, Celia Ravenscroft, the other day,' said Mrs Oliver. 'Do you remember the Ravenscrofts? Of course, it's a great many years ago.'

'The Ravenscrofts? Now wait a minute. That was that very sad tragedy, wasn't it? A double suicide, didn't they think it was? Near their house at Overcliffe.'

'You've got such a wonderful memory, Julia,' said Mrs Oliver.

'Always had. Though I have difficulties with names sometimes. Yes, it was very tragic, wasn't it.'

'Very tragic indeed.'

'One of my cousins knew them very well in Malaya, Roddy Foster, you know. General Ravenscroft had had a most distinguished career. Of course he was a bit deaf by the time he retired. He didn't always hear what one said very well.'

'Do you remember them quite well?'

'Oh yes. One doesn't really forget people, does one? I mean, they lived at Overcliffe for quite five or six years.'

'I've forgotten her Christian name now,' said Mrs Oliver.

'Margaret, I think. But everyone called her Molly. Yes, Margaret. So many people were called Margaret, weren't they, at about that time? She used to wear a wig, do you remember?'

'Oh yes,' said Mrs Oliver. 'At least I can't quite remember, but I think I do.'

'I'm not sure she didn't try to persuade me to get one. She said it was so useful when you went abroad and travelled. She had four different wigs. One for evening and one for travelling and one – very strange, you know. You could put a hat on over it and not really disarrange it.'

'I didn't know them as well as you did,' said Mrs Oliver. 'And of course at the time of the shooting I was in America on a lecture tour. So I never really heard any details.'

'Well, of course, it was a great mystery,' said Julia Carstairs. 'I mean to say, one didn't know. There were so many different stories going about.'

'What did they say at the inquest – I suppose they had an inquest?'

'Oh yes, of course. The police had to investigate it. It was one of those indecisive things, you know, in that the death was due to revolver shots. They couldn't say definitely what had occurred. It seemed possible that General Ravenscroft had shot his wife and then himself, but apparently it was just as probable that Lady Ravenscroft had shot her husband and then herself. It seemed more likely, I think, that it *was* a suicide pact, but it couldn't be said definitely how it came about.'

'There seemed to be no question of its being a crime?'

'No, no. It was said quite clearly there was no suggestion of foul play. I mean there were no footprints or any signs of anyone coming near them. They left the house to go for a walk after tea, as they so often did. They didn't come back again for dinner and the manservant or somebody or the gardener – whoever it was – went out to look for them, and found them both dead. The revolver was lying by the bodies.'

'The revolver belonged to him, didn't it?'

'Oh yes. He had two revolvers in the house. These ex-military people so often do, don't they? I mean, they feel safer what with everything that goes on nowadays. A second revolver was still in the drawer in the house, so that he – well, *he* must have gone out deliberately with the revolver, presumably. I don't think it likely that she'd have gone out for a walk carrying a revolver.'

'No. No, it wouldn't have been so easy, would it?'

'But there was nothing apparently in the evidence to show that there was any unhappiness or that there'd been any quarrel between them or that there was any reason why they should commit suicide. Of course one never knows what sad things there are in people's lives.'

'No, no,' said Mrs Oliver. 'One never knows. How very true that is, Julia. Did you have any ideas yourself?'

'Well, one always wonders, my dear.'

'Yes,' said Mrs Oliver, 'one always wonders.'

'It might be of course, you see, that he had some disease. I think he might have been told he was going to die of cancer, but that wasn't so, according to the medical evidence. He was quite healthy. I mean, he had – I think he had had a – what do they call those things? – coronary, is that what I mean? It sounds like a crown, doesn't it, but it's really a heart attack, isn't it? He'd had that but he'd recovered from it, and she was, well, she was very nervy. She was neurotic always.'

'Yes, I seem to remember that,' said Mrs Oliver. 'Of course I didn't know them well, but – ' she asked suddenly – 'was she wearing a wig?'

'Oh. Well, you know, I can't really remember that. She always wore her wig. One of them, I mean.'

'I just wondered,' said Mrs Oliver. 'Somehow I feel if you were going to shoot yourself or even shoot your husband, I don't think you'd wear your wig, do you?'

The ladies discussed this point with some interest.

'What do you really think, Julia?'

'Well, as I said, dear, one wonders, you know. There were things said, but then there always are.'

'About him or her?'

'Well, they said that there was a young woman, you know. Yes, I think she did some secretarial work for him. He was writing his memoirs of his career abroad – I believe commissioned by a publisher at that – and she used to take dictation from him. But some people said – well, you know what they do say sometimes, that perhaps he had got – er – tied up with this girl in some way. She wasn't very young. She was over thirty, and not very good-looking and I don't think – there were no scandals about her or anything, but still, one doesn't know. People thought he might have shot his wife because he wanted to – well, he might have wanted to marry her, yes. But I don't really think people said that sort of thing and *I* never believed it.'

'What did you think?'

'Well, of course I wondered a little about *her*.'

'You mean that a man was mentioned?'

'I believe there was something out in Malaya. Some kind of story I heard about her. That she got embroiled with some young man much younger than herself. And her husband hadn't liked it much and it had caused a bit of scandal. I forget where. But anyway, that was a long time ago and I don't think anything ever came of it.'

'You don't think there was any talk nearer home? No special relationship with anyone in the neighbourhood? There wasn't any evidence of quarrels between them, or anything of that kind?'

'No, I don't think so. Of course I read everything about it at the time. One did discuss it, of course, because one couldn't help feeling there might be some – well, some really very tragic love story connected with it.'

'But there wasn't, you think? They had children, didn't they. There was my goddaughter, of course.'

'Oh yes, and there was a son. I think he was quite young. At school somewhere. The girl was only twelve, no – older than that. She was with a family in Switzerland.'

'There was no – no mental trouble, I suppose, in the family?'

'Oh, you mean the boy – yes, *might* be of course. You do hear very strange things. There was that boy who shot his father – that was somewhere near Newcastle, I think. Some years before that. You know. He'd been very depressed and at first I think they said he tried to hang himself when he was at the university, and then he came and shot his father. But nobody quite knew why. Anyway, there wasn't anything of that sort with the Ravenscrofts. No, I don't think so, in fact I'm pretty sure of it. I can't help thinking, in some ways –'

'Yes, Julia?'

'I can't help thinking that there might have been a man, you know.'

'You mean that she –?'

'Yes, well – well, one thinks it rather likely, you know. The wigs, for one thing.'

'I don't quite see how the wigs come into it.'

'Well, wanting to improve her appearance.'

'She was thirty-five, I think.'

'More. More. Thirty-six, I think. And, well, I know she showed me the wigs one day, and one or two of them really made her look quite attractive. And she used a good deal of make-up. And that had all started just after they had come to live there, I think. She was rather a good-looking woman.'

'You mean, she might have met someone, some man?'

'Well, that's what I've always thought,' said Mrs Carstairs. 'You see, if a man's getting off with a girl, people notice it usually because men aren't so good at hiding their tracks. But a woman, it might be – well, I mean like someone she'd met and nobody knew much about it.'

'Oh, do you really think so, Julia?'

'No I don't really think so,' said Julia, 'because I mean, people always do know, don't they? I mean, you know, servants know, or gardeners or bus drivers. Or somebody in the neighbourhood. And they know. And they talk. But still, there could have been something like that, and either he found out about it . . .'

'You mean it was a crime of jealousy?'

'I think so, yes.'

'So you think it's more likely that he shot her, then himself, than that she shot him and then herself.'

'Well, I should think so, because I think if she were trying to get rid of him – well, I don't think they'd have gone for a walk together and she'd have to have taken the revolver with her in a handbag and it would have been rather a bigger handbag if so. One has to think of the practical side of things.'

'I know,' said Mrs Oliver. 'One does. It's very interesting.'

'It must be interesting to you, dear, because you write these crime stories. So I expect really you would have better ideas. You'd know more what's likely to happen.'

'I don't know what's likely to happen,' said Mrs Oliver, 'because, you see, in all the crimes that I write, I've invented the crimes. I mean, what I want to happen, happens in my stories. It's not something that actually has happened or that could happen. So I'm really the worst person to talk about it. I'm interested to know what you think because you know people very well, Julia, and you knew them well. And I think she might have said something to you one day – or he might.'

'Yes. Yes, now wait a minute when you say that, that seems to bring something back to me.'

Mrs Carstairs leaned back in her chair, shook her head doubtfully, half closed her eyes and went into a kind of coma. Mrs Oliver remained silent with a look on her face which women are apt to wear when they are waiting for the first signs of a kettle coming to the boil.

'She did say something once, I remember, and I wonder what she meant by it,' said Mrs Carstairs. 'Something about starting a new life – in connection I think with St Teresa. St Teresa of Avila.'

Mrs Oliver looked slightly startled.

'But how did St Teresa of Avila come into it?'

'Well, I don't know really. I think she must have been reading a Life of her. Anyway, she said that it was wonderful how women get a sort of second wind. That's not quite the term she used, but something like that. You know, when they are forty or fifty or that sort of age and they suddenly want to begin a new life. Teresa of Avila did. She hadn't done anything special up till then except being a nun, then she went out and reformed all the convents, didn't she, and flung her weight about and became a great Saint.'

'Yes, but that doesn't seem quite the same thing.'

'No, it doesn't,' said Mrs Carstairs. 'But women do talk in a very silly way, you know, when they are referring to love-affairs when they get on in life. About how it's never too late.'

Chapter 7

BACK TO THE NURSERY

Mrs Oliver looked rather doubtfully at the three steps and the front door of a small, rather dilapidated-looking cottage in the side street. Below the windows some bulbs were growing, mainly tulips.

Mrs Oliver paused, opened the little address book in her hand, verified that she was in the place she thought she was, and rapped gently with the knocker after having tried to press a bell-push of possible electrical significance but which did not seem to yield any satisfactory bell ringing inside, or anything of that kind. Presently, not getting any response, she knocked again. This time there were sounds from inside. A shuffling sound of feet, some asthmatic breathing and hands apparently trying to manage the opening of the door. With this noise there came a few vague echoes in the letter-box.

'Oh, drat it. Drat it. Stuck again, you brute, you.'

Finally, success met these inward industries, and the door, making a creaky and rather doubtful noise, was slowly pulled open. A very old woman with a wrinkled face, humped shoulders and a general arthritic appearance, looked at her visitor. Her face was unwelcoming. It held no sign of fear, merely of distaste for those who came and knocked at the home of an Englishwoman's castle. She might have been seventy or eighty, but she was still a valiant defender of her home.

'I dunno what you've come about and I–' she stopped. 'Why,' she said, 'it's Miss Ariadne. Well I never now! It's Miss Ariadne.'

'I think you're wonderful to know me,' said Mrs Oliver. 'How are you, Mrs Matcham?'

'Miss Ariadne! Just think of that now.'

It was, Mrs Ariadne Oliver thought, a long time ago since she had been addressed as Miss Ariadne, but the intonation of the voice, cracked with age though it was, rang a familiar note.

'Come in, m'dear,' said the old dame, 'come in now. You're lookin' well, you are. I dunno how many years it is since I've seen you. Fifteen at least.'

It was a good deal more than fifteen but Mrs Oliver made no corrections. She came in. Mrs Matcham was shaking hands, her hands were rather unwilling to obey their owner's orders. She managed to shut the door and, shuffling her feet and limping, entered a small room which was obviously one that was kept for the reception of any likely or unlikely visitors whom Mrs Matcham was prepared to admit to her home. There were large numbers of photographs, some of babies, some of adults. Some in nice leather frames which were slowly drooping but had not quite fallen to pieces yet. One in a silver frame by now rather tarnished, representing a young woman in presentation Court Dress with feathers rising up on her head. Two naval officers, two military gentlemen, some photographs of naked babies sprawling on rugs. There was a sofa and two chairs. As bidden, Mrs Oliver sat in a chair. Mrs Matcham pressed herself down on the sofa and pulled a cushion into the hollow of her back with some difficulty.

'Well, my dear, fancy seeing you. And you're still writing your pretty stories, are you?'

'Yes,' said Mrs Oliver, assenting to this though with a slight doubt as to how far detective stories and stories of crime and general criminal behaviour could be called 'pretty stories'. But that, she thought, was very much a habit of Mrs Matcham's.

'I'm all alone now,' said Mrs Matcham. 'You remember Gracie, my sister? She died last autumn, she did. Cancer it was. They operated but it was too late.'

'Oh dear, I'm so sorry,' said Mrs Oliver.

Conversation proceeded for the next ten minutes on the subject of the demise, one by one, of Mrs Matcham's last remaining relatives.

'And you're all right, are you? Doing all right? Got a husband now? Oh now, I remember, he's dead years ago, isn't he? And what brings you here, to Little Saltern Minor?'

'I just happened to be in the neighbourhood,' said Mrs Oliver, 'and as I've got your address in my little address book with me, I thought I'd just drop in and – well, see how you were and everything.'

'Ah! And talk about old times, perhaps. Always nice when you can do that, isn't it?'

'Yes, indeed,' said Mrs Oliver, feeling some relief that this particular line had been indicated to her since it was more or less what she had come for. 'What a lot of photographs you've got,' she said.

'Ah, I have, an' that. D'you know, when I was in that Home – silly name it had, Sunset House of Happiness for the Aged, something like that it was called, a year and a quarter I lived there till I couldn't stand it no more, a nasty lot they were, saying you couldn't have any of your own things with you. You know, everything had to belong to the Home. I don't say as it wasn't comfortable, but you know, I like me own things around me. My photos and my furniture. And then there was ever so nice a lady, came from a Council she did, some society or other, and she told me there was another place where they had homes of their own or something and you could take what you liked with you. And there's ever such a nice helper as comes in every day to see if you're all right. Ah, very comfortable I am here. Very comfortable indeed. I've got all my own things.'

'Something from everywhere,' said Mrs Oliver, looking round.

'Yes, that table – the brass one – that's Captain Wilson, he sent me that from Singapore or something like that. And that Benares brass too. That's nice, isn't it? That's a funny thing on the ashtray. That's Egyptian, that is. It's a scarabee, or some name like that. You know. Sounds like some kind of scratching disease but it isn't. No, it's a sort of beetle and it's made out of some stone. They call it a precious stone. Bright blue. A lazy – a lavis – a lazy lapin or something like that.'

'Lapis lazuli,' said Mrs Oliver.

'That's right. That's what it is. Very nice, that is. That was my archaeological boy what went digging. He sent me that.'

'All your lovely past,' said Mrs Oliver.

'Yes, all my boys and girls. Some of them as babies, some of them I had from the month, and the older ones. Some of them when I went to India and that other time when I was in Siam. Yes. That's Miss Moya in her Court dress. Ah, she was a pretty thing. Divorced two husbands, she has. Yes. Trouble with his lordship, the first one, and then she married one of those pop singers and of course that couldn't take very well. And then she married someone in California. They had a yacht and went places, I think. Died two or three years ago and only sixty-two. Pity dying so young, you know.'

'You've been to a lot of different parts of the world yourself, haven't you?' said Mrs Oliver. 'India, Hong Kong, then Egypt, and South America, wasn't it?'

'Ah yes, I've been about a good deal.'

'I remember,' said Mrs Oliver, 'when I was in Malaya, you were with a service family then, weren't you? A General somebody. Was it – now wait a minute, I can't remember the name – it wasn't General and Lady Ravenscroft, was it?'

'No, no, you've got the name wrong. You're thinking of when I was with the Barnabys. That's right. You came to stay with them. Remember? You were doing a tour, you were, and you came and stayed with the Barnabys. You were an old friend of hers. He was a Judge.'

'Ah yes,' said Mrs Oliver. 'It's difficult a bit. One gets names mixed up.'

'Two nice children they had,' said Mrs Matcham. 'Of course they went to school in England. The boy went to Harrow and the girl went to Roedean, I think it was, and so I moved on to another family after that. Ah, things have changed nowadays. Not so many amahs, even, as there used to be. Mind you, the amahs used to be a bit of a trouble now and then. I got on with our one very well when I was with the Barnabys, I mean. Who was it you spoke of? The Ravenscrofts? Well, I remember them. Yes – I forget the name of the place where they lived now. Not far from us. The families were acquainted, you know. Oh yes, it's a long time ago, but I remember it all. I was still out there with the Barnabys, you know. I stayed on when the children went to school to look after Mrs Barnaby. Look after her things, you know, and mend them and all that. Oh yes, I was there when that awful thing happened. I don't mean the Barnabys, I mean to the Ravenscrofts. Yes, I shall never forget that. Hearing about it, I mean. Naturally I wasn't mixed up in it myself, but it was a terrible thing to happen, wasn't it?'

'I should think it must have been,' said Mrs Oliver.

'It was after you'd gone back to England, a good long time after that, I think. A nice couple they were. Very nice couple and it was a shock to them.'

'I don't really remember now,' said Mrs Oliver.

'I know. One forgets things. I don't myself. But they said she'd always been queer, you know. Ever since the time she was a child. Some early story there was. She took a baby out of the pram and threw it in the river. Jealousy, they said. Other people said she wanted the baby to go to heaven and not wait.'

'Is it – is it Lady Ravenscroft, you mean?'

'No, of course I don't. Ah, you don't remember as well as I do. It was the sister.'

'Her sister?'

'I'm not sure now whether it was her sister or his sister. They said she'd been in a kind of mental place for a long time, you know. Ever since she was about eleven or twelve years old. They kept her there and then they said she was all right again and she came out. And she married some-one in the Army. And then there was trouble. And the next thing they heard, I believe, was that she'd been put back again in one of them loony-bin places. They treat you very well, you know. They have a suite, nice rooms and all that. And they used to go and see her, I believe. I mean the General did or his wife. The children were brought up by someone else, I think, because they were afraid-like. However, they said she was all right in the end. So she came back to live with her husband, and then he died or something. Blood pressure I think it was, or heart. Anyway, she was very upset and she came out to stay with her brother or her sister – whichever it was – she seemed quite happy there and everything, and ever so fond of children, she was. It wasn't the little boy, I think, he was at school. It was the little girl, and another little girl who'd come to play with her that afternoon. Ah well, I can't remember the details now. It's so long ago. There was a lot of talk about it. There was some as said, you know, as it wasn't her at all. They thought it was the amah that had done it, but the amah loved them and she was very, very upset. She wanted to take them away from the house. She said they weren't safe there, and all sorts of things like that. But of course the others didn't believe in it and then this came about and I gather they think it must have been whatever her name was – I can't remember it now. Anyway, there it was.'

'And what happened to this sister, either of General or Lady Ravenscroft?'

'Well, I think, you know, as she was taken away by a doctor and put in some place and went back to England, I believe, in the end. I dunno if she went to the same place as before, but she was well looked after somewhere. There was plenty of money, I think, you know. Plenty of money in the husband's family. Maybe she got all right again. But well, I haven't thought of it for years. Not till you came here asking me stories about General and Lady Ravenscroft. I wonder where they are now. They must have retired before now, long ago.'

'Well, it was rather sad,' said Mrs Oliver. 'Perhaps you read about it in the papers.'

'Read what?'

'Well, they bought a house in England and then –'

'Ah now, it's coming back to me. I remember reading something about that in the paper. Yes, and thinking then that I knew the name Ravenscroft, but I couldn't quite remember when and how. They fell over a cliff, didn't they? Something of that kind.'

'Yes,' said Mrs Oliver, 'something of that kind.'

'Now look here, dearie, it's so nice to see you, it is. You must let me give you a cup of tea.'

'Really,' said Mrs Oliver, 'I don't need any tea. Really, I don't want it.'

'Of course you want some tea. If you don't mind now, come into the kitchen, will you? I mean, I spend most of my time there now. It's easier to get about there. But I take visitors always into this room because I'm proud of my things, you know. Proud of my things and proud of all the children and the others.'

'I think,' said Mrs Oliver, 'that people like you must have had a wonderful life with all the children you've looked after.'

'Yes. I remember when you were a little girl, you liked

to listen to the stories I told you. There was one about a tiger, I remember, and one about monkeys – monkeys in a tree.'

'Yes,' said Mrs Oliver, 'I remember those. It was a very long time ago.'

Her mind swept back to herself, a child of six or seven, walking in button boots that were rather too tight on a road in England, and listening to a story of India and Egypt from an attendant Nanny. And this was Nanny. Mrs Matcham was Nanny. She looked round the room as she followed her hostess out. At the pictures of girls, of schoolboys, of children and various middle-aged people, all mainly photographed in their best clothes and sent in nice frames or other things because they hadn't forgotten Nanny. Because of them, probably, Nanny was having a reasonably comfortable old age with money supplied. Mrs Oliver felt a sudden desire to burst out crying. This was so unlike her that she was able to stop herself by an effort of will. She followed Mrs Matcham to the kitchen. There she produced the offering she had brought.

'Well, I never! A tin of Tophole Thathams tea. Always my favourite. Fancy you remembering. I can hardly ever get it nowadays. And that's my favourite tea biscuits. Well, you are a one for never forgetting. What was it they used to call you – those two little boys who came to play – one would call you Lady Elephant and the other one called you Lady Swan. The one who called you Lady Elephant used to sit on your back and you went about the floor on all fours and pretended to have a trunk you picked things up with.'

'You don't forget many things, do you, Nanny?' said Mrs Oliver.

'Ah,' said Mrs Matcham. 'Elephants don't forget. That's the old saying.'

Chapter 8

MRS OLIVER AT WORK

Mrs Oliver entered the premises of Williams & Barnet, a well-appointed chemist's shop also dealing with various cosmetics. She paused by a kind of dumb waiter containing various types of corn remedies, hesitated by a mountain of rubber sponges, wandered vaguely towards the prescription desk and then came down past the well-displayed aids to beauty as imagined by Elizabeth Arden, Helena Rubinstein, Max Factor and other benefit providers for women's lives.

She stopped finally near a rather plump girl and enquired for certain lipsticks, then uttered a short cry of surprise.

'Why, Marlene – it is Marlene isn't it?'

'Well, I never. It's Mrs Oliver. I am pleased to see you. It's wonderful, isn't it? All the girls will be very excited when I tell them that you've been in to buy things here.'

'No need to tell them,' said Mrs Oliver.

'Oh, now I'm sure they'll be bringing out their autograph books!'

'I'd rather they didn't,' said Mrs Oliver. 'And how are you, Marlene?'

'Oh, getting along, getting along,' said Marlene.

'I didn't know whether you'd be working here still.'

'Well, it's as good as any other place, I think, and they treat you very well here, you know. I had a rise in salary last year and I'm more or less in charge of this cosmetic counter now.'

'And your mother? Is she well?'

'Oh yes. Mum will be pleased to hear I've met you.'

'Is she still living in her same house down the – the road past the hospital?'

'Oh yes, we're still there. Dad's not been so well. He's been in hospital for a while, but Mum keeps along very well indeed. Oh, she will be pleased to hear I've seen you. Are you staying here by any chance?'

'Not really,' said Mrs Oliver. 'I'm just passing through, as a matter of fact. I've been to see an old friend and I wonder now – ' she looked at her wrist-watch. 'Would your mother be at home now, Marlene? I could just call in and see her. Have a few words before I have to get on.'

'Oh, do do that,' said Marlene. 'She'd be ever so pleased. I'm sorry I can't leave here and come with you, but I don't think – well, it wouldn't be viewed very well. You know I can't get off for another hour and a half.'

'Oh well, some other time,' said Mrs Oliver. 'Anyway, I can't quite remember – was it number 17 or has it got a name?'

'It's called Laurel Cottage.'

'Oh yes, of course. How stupid of me. Well, nice to have seen you.'

She hurried out plus one unwanted lipstick in her bag, and drove her car down the main street of Chipping Bartram and turned, after passing a garage and a hospital building, down a rather narrow road which had quite pleasant small houses on either side of it.

She left the car outside Laurel Cottage and went in. A thin, energetic woman with grey hair, of about fifty years of age, opened the door and displayed instant signs of recognition.

'Why, so it's you, Mrs Oliver. Ah well, now. Not seen you for years and years, I haven't.'

'Oh, it's a very long time.'

'Well, come in then, come in. Can I make you a nice cup of tea?'

'I'm afraid not,' said Mrs Oliver, 'because I've had tea already with a friend, and I've got to get back to London. As it happened, I went into the chemist for something I wanted and I saw Marlene there.'

'Yes, she's got a very good job there. They think a lot of her in that place. They say she's got a lot of enterprise.'

'Well, that's very nice. And how are you, Mrs Buckle? You look very well. Hardly older than when I saw you last.'

'Oh, I wouldn't like to say that. Grey hairs, and I've lost a lot of weight.'

'This seems to be a day when I meet a lot of friends I knew formerly,' said Mrs Oliver, going into the house and being led into a small, rather over-cluttered sitting-room. 'I don't know if you remember Mrs Carstairs – Mrs Julia Carstairs.'

'Oh, of course I do. Yes, rather. She must be getting on.'

'Oh yes, she is, really. But we talked over a few old

days, you know. In fact, we went as far as talking about that tragedy that occurred. I was in America at the time so I didn't know much about it. People called Ravenscroft.'

'Oh, I remember that well.'

'You worked for them, didn't you, at one time, Mrs Buckle?'

'Yes. I used to go in three mornings a week. Very nice people they were. You know, real military lady and gentleman, as you might say. The old school.'

'It was a very tragic thing to happen.'

'Yes, it was, indeed.'

'Were you still working for them at that time?'

'No. As a matter of fact, I'd given up going there. I had my old Aunt Emma come to live with me and she was rather blind and not very well, and I couldn't really spare the time any more to go out doing things for people. But I'd been with them up to about a month or two before that.'

'It seemed such a terrible thing to happen,' said Mrs Oliver. 'I understand that they thought it was a suicide pact.'

'I don't believe that,' said Mrs Buckle. 'I'm sure they'd never have committed suicide together. Not people like that. And living so pleasantly together as they did. Of course, they hadn't lived there very long.'

'No, I suppose they hadn't,' said Mrs Oliver. 'They lived somewhere near Bournemouth, didn't they, when they first came to England?'

'Yes, but they found it was a bit too far for getting to London from there, and so that's why they came to Chipping Bartram. Very nice house it was, and a nice garden.'

'Were they both in good health when you were working for them last?'

'Well, he felt his age a bit as most people do. The General, he'd had some kind of heart trouble or a slight stroke. Something of that kind, you know. They'd take pills, you know, and lie up a bit from time to time.'

'And Lady Ravenscroft?'

'Well, I think she missed the life she'd had abroad, you know. They didn't know so very many people there, although they got to know a good many families, of course, being the sort of class they were. But I suppose it wasn't like Malaya or those places. You know, where you have a lot of servants. I suppose gay parties and that sort of thing.'

'You think she missed her gay parties?'

'Well, I don't know that exactly.'

'Somebody told me she'd taken to wearing a wig.'

'Oh, she'd got several wigs,' said Mrs Buckle, smiling slightly. 'Very smart ones and very expensive. You know, from time to time she'd send one back to the place she'd got it from in London, and they'd re-dress it for her again and send it. There were all kinds. You know, there was one with auburn hair, and one with little grey curls all over her head. Really, she looked very nice in that one. And two – well, not so attractive really but useful for – you know – windy days when you wanted something to put on when it might be raining. Thought a lot about her appearance, you know and spent a lot of her money on clothes.'

'What do you think was the cause of the tragedy?' said Mrs Oliver. 'You see, not being anywhere near here and not seeing any of my friends at that time because I was in America, I missed hearing anything about it and, well, one doesn't like to ask questions or write letters about things of that kind. I suppose there must have been some cause. I mean, it was General Ravenscroft's own revolver that was used, I understand.'

'Oh yes, he had two of those in the house because he said that no house was safe without. Perhaps he was right there, you know. Not that they'd had any trouble beforehand as far as I know. One afternoon a rather nasty sort of fellow came along to the door. Didn't like the look of him, I didn't. Wanted to see the General. Said he'd been in the General's regiment when he was a young fellow. The General asked him a few questions and I think thought as how he didn't – well, thought he wasn't very reliable. So he sent him off.'

'You think then that it was someone outside that did it?'

'Well, I think it must have been because I can't see any other thing. Mind you, I didn't like the man who came and did the gardening for them very much. He hadn't got a very good reputation and I gather he'd had a few jail sentences earlier in his life. But of course the General took up his references and he wanted to give him a chance.'

'So you think the gardener might have killed them?'

'Well, I – I always thought that. But then I'm probably wrong. But it doesn't seem to me – I mean, the people who said there was some scandalous story or something about either her or him and that either he'd shot her or

73

she'd shot him, that's all nonsense, I'd say. No, it was some outsider. One of these people that – well, it's not as bad as it is nowadays because that, you must remember, was before people began getting all this violence idea. But look at what you read in the papers every day now. Young men, practically only boys still, taking a lot of drugs and going wild and rushing about, shooting a lot of people for nothing at all, asking a girl in a pub to have a drink with them and then they see her home and next day her body's found in a ditch. Stealing children out of prams from their mothers, taking a girl to a dance and murdering her or strangling her on the way back. If anything, you feel as anyone can do anything. And anyway, there's that nice couple, the General and his wife, out for a nice walk in the evening, and there they were, both shot through the head.'

'Was it through the head?'

'Well, I don't remember exactly now and of course I never saw anything myself. But anyway, just went for a walk as they often did.'

'And they'd not been on bad terms with each other?'

'Well, they had words now and again, but who doesn't?'

'No boy-friend or girl-friend?'

'Well, if you can use that term of people of that age, oh, I mean there was a bit of talk here and there, but it was all nonsense. Nothing to it at all. People always want to say something of that kind.'

'Perhaps one of them was – ill.'

'Well, Lady Ravenscroft had been up to London once or twice consulting a doctor about something and I rather think she was going into hospital, or planning to go into hospital for an operation of some kind though she never told me exactly what it was. But I think they managed to put her right – she was in this hospital for a short time. No operation, I think. And when she came back she looked very much younger. Altogether, she'd had a lot of face treatment and you know, she looked so pretty in these wigs with curls on them. Rather as though she'd got a new lease of life.'

'And General Ravenscroft?'

'He was a very nice gentleman and I never heard or knew of any scandal about him and I don't think there was any. People say things, but then they want to say something when there's been a tragedy of any kind. It seems to me perhaps as he might have had a blow on the head in Malaya or something like that. I had an uncle or a great-uncle, you know, who fell off his horse there once. Hit it on a cannon or something and he was very queer afterwards. All right for about six months and then they had to put him into an asylum because he wanted to take his wife's life the whole time. He said she was persecuting him and following him and that she was a spy for another nation. Ah, there's no saying what things happen or can happen in families.'

'Anyway, you don't think there was any truth in some of the stories about them that I have happened to hear of, bad feeling between them so that one of them shot the other and then shot himself or herself.'

'Oh no, I don't.'

'Were her children at home at the time?'

'No. Miss – er – oh what was her name now, Rosie? No. Penelope?'

'Celia,' said Mrs Oliver. 'She's my goddaughter.'

'Oh, of course she is. Yes, I know that now. I remember you coming and taking her out once. She was a high-spirited girl, rather bad-tempered in some ways, but she was very fond of her father and mother, I think. No, she was away at a school in Switzerland when it happened, I'm glad to say, because it would have been a terrible shock to her if she'd been at home and the one who saw them.'

'And there was a boy, too, wasn't there?'

'Oh yes. Master Edward. His father was a bit worried about him, I think. He looked as though he disliked his father.'

'Oh, there's nothing in that. Boys go through that stage. Was he very devoted to his mother?'

'Well, she fussed over him a bit too much, I think, which he found tiresome. You know, they don't like a mother fussing over them, telling them to wear thicker vests or put an extra pullover on. His father, he didn't like the way he wore his hair. It was – well they weren't wearing hair like the way they are nowadays, but they were beginning to, if you know what I mean.'

'But the boy wasn't at home at the time of the tragedy?'

'No.'

'I suppose it was a shock to him?'

'Well, it must have been. Of course, I wasn't going to the house any more at that time so I didn't hear so much. If you ask me, I didn't like that gardener. What was his name now – Fred, I think. Fred Wizell. Some name like that. Seems to me if he'd done a bit of – well, a bit of cheating or something like that and the General had found him out and was going to sack him, I wouldn't put it past him.'

'To shoot the husband and wife?'

'Well, I'd have thought it more likely he'd just have shot the General. If he shot the General and the wife came along, then he'd have had to shoot her too. You read things like that in books.'

'Yes,' said Mrs Oliver thoughtfully, 'one does read all sorts of things in books.'

'There was the tutor. I didn't like him much.'

'What tutor?'

'Well, there was a tutor for the boy earlier. You know, he couldn't pass an exam and things at the earlier school he was at – prep school or something. So they had a tutor for him. He was there for about a year, I think. Lady Ravenscroft liked him very much. She was musical, you know, and so was this tutor. Mr Edmunds, I think his name was. Rather a namby-pamby sort of young man, I thought myself, and it's my opinion that General Ravenscroft didn't care for him much.'

'But Lady Ravenscroft did.'

'Oh, they had a lot in common, I think. And I think she was the one really that chose him rather more than the General. Mind you, he had very nice manners and spoke to everyone nicely and all that – '

'And did – what's-his-name?'

'Edward? Oh yes, he liked him all right, I think. In fact, he was quite a bit soft on him, I think. Almost a bit of hero-worship. Anyway, don't you believe any stories you hear about scandals in the family or her having an affair with anyone or General Ravenscroft with that rather pi-faced girl who did filing work for him and all that sort of thing. No. Whoever that wicked murderer was, it's one who came from outside. The police never got on to anyone, a car was seen near there but there was nothing to it and they never got any further. But all the same I think one ought to look about for somebody perhaps who'd known them in Malaya or abroad or somewhere else, or even when they were first living at Bournemouth. One never knows.'

'What did your husband think about it?' said Mrs Oliver. 'He wouldn't have known as much about them as you would, of course, but still he might have heard a lot.'

'Oh, he heard a lot of talk, of course. In the George and Flag, of an evening, you know. People saying all sorts of things. Said as she drank and that cases of empty bottles had been taken out of the house. Absolutely untrue, that was, I know for a fact. And there was a nephew as used to come and see them sometimes. Got into trouble with the police in some way, he did, but I don't think there was anything in that. The police didn't, either. Anyway, it wasn't at that time.'

'There was no one else really living in the house, was there, except the General and Lady Ravenscroft?'

'Well, she had a sister as used to come sometimes, Lady Ravenscroft did. She was a half-sister, I think. Something like that. Looked rather like Lady Ravenscroft. She made a bit of trouble between them, I always used to think, when she came for a visit. She was one of those who likes stirring things up, if you know what I mean. Just said things to annoy people.'

'Was Lady Ravenscroft fond of her?'

'Well, if you ask me, I don't think she was really. I think the sister more or less wished herself on to them sometimes and she didn't like not to have her, but I think she found it pretty trying to have her there. The General quite liked her because she played cards well. Played chess and things with him and he enjoyed that. And she was an amusing woman in a way. Mrs Jerryboy or something like that, her name was. She was a widow, I think. Used to borrow money from them, I think, too.'

'Did you like her?'

'Well, if you don't mind my saying so, ma'am, no, I didn't like her. I disliked her very much. I thought she was one of those trouble-makers, you know. But she hadn't been down for some time before the tragedy happened. I don't really remember very much what she was like. She had a son as came with her once or twice. Didn't like him very much. Shifty, I thought.'

'Well,' said Mrs Oliver. 'I suppose nobody will really ever know the truth. Not now. Not after all this time. I saw my goddaughter the other day.'

'Did you now, ma'am. I'd be interested to hear about Miss Celia. How is she? All right?'

'Yes. She seems quite all right. I think she's thinking

perhaps of getting married. At any rate she's got a – '

'Got a steady boy-friend, has she?' said Mrs Buckle. 'Ah well, we've all got that. Not that we all marry the first one we settle on. Just as well if you don't, nine times out of ten.'

'You don't know a Mrs Burton-Cox, do you?' asked Mrs Oliver.

'Burton-Cox? I seem to know that name. No, I don't think so. Wasn't living down here or come to stay with them or anything? No, not that I remember. Yet I did hear something. Some old friend of General Ravenscroft, I think, which he'd known in Malaya. But I don't know.' She shook her head.

'Well,' said Mrs Oliver, 'I mustn't stay gossiping with you any longer. It's been so nice to see you and Marlene.'

Chapter 9

RESULTS OF
ELEPHANTINE RESEARCH

'A telephone call for you,' said Hercule Poirot's manservant, George. 'From Mrs Oliver.'

'Ah yes, George. And what had she to say?'

'She wondered if she could come and see you this evening, sir, after dinner.'

'That would be admirable,' said Poirot. 'Admirable. I have had a tiring day. It will be a stimulating experience to see Mrs Oliver. She is always entertaining as well as being highly unexpected in the things she says. Did she mention elephants, by the way?'

'Elephants, sir? No, I do not think so.'

'Ah. Then it would seem perhaps that the elephants have been disappointing.'

George looked at his master rather doubtfully. There were times when he did not quite understand the relevance of Poirot's remarks.

'Ring her back,' said Hercule Poirot, 'tell her I shall be delighted to receive her.'

George went away to carry out this order, and returned to say that Mrs Oliver would be there about quarter to nine.

'Coffee,' said Poirot. 'Let coffee be prepared and some *petit-fours*. I rather think I ordered some in lately from Fortnum and Mason.'

'A liqueur of any kind, sir?'

'No, I think not. I myself will have some *Sirop de Cassis*.'

'Yes, sir.'

Mrs Oliver arrived exactly on time. Poirot greeted her with every sign of pleasure.

'And how are you, *chère madame*?'

'Exhausted,' said Mrs Oliver.

She sank down into the armchair that Poirot indicated.

'Completely exhausted.'

'Ah. *Qui va à la chasse* – oh, I cannot remember the saying.'

'I remember it,' said Mrs Oliver. 'I learnt it as a child. "*Qui va à la chasse perd sa place*."'

'That, I am sure, is not applicable to the chase you have been conducting. I am referring to the pursuit of elephants, unless that was merely a figure of speech.'

'Not at all,' said Mrs Oliver. 'I have been pursuing elephants madly. Here, there and everywhere. The amount of petrol I have used, the amount of trains I have taken, the amount of letters I've written, the amount of telegrams I've sent – you wouldn't believe how exhausting it all is.'

'Then repose yourself. Have some coffee.'

'Nice, strong, black coffee – yes, I will. Just what I want.'

'Did you, may I ask, get any results?'

'Plenty of results,' said Mrs Oliver. 'The trouble is, I don't know whether any of them are any use.'

'You learn facts, however?'

'No. Not really. I learnt things that people told me were facts, but I strongly doubt myself whether any of them *were* facts.'

'They were hearsay?'

'No. They were what I said they would be. They were memories. Lots of people who had memories. The trouble is, when you remember things you don't always remember them right, do you?'

'No. But they are still what you might describe perhaps as results. Is not that so?'

'And what have you done?' said Mrs Oliver.

'You are always so stern, madame,' said Poirot. 'You demand that I run about, that I also do things.'

'Well, have you run about?'

'I have not run about, but I have had a few consultations with others of my own profession.'

'It sounds far more peaceful than what I have been doing,' said Mrs Oliver. 'Oh, this coffee is nice. It's really strong. You wouldn't believe how tired I am. And how muddled.'

'Come, come. Let us have good expectancy. You have got things. You have got something, I think.'

'I've got a lot of different suggestions and stories. I don't know whether any of them are true.'

'They could be not true, but still be of use,' said Poirot.

'Well, I know what you mean,' said Mrs Oliver, 'and that's what I think, too. I mean, that's what I thought when I went about it. When people remember something and tell you about it – I mean, it's often not quite actually what occurred, but it's what they themselves thought occurred.'

'But they must have had something on which to base it,' said Poirot.

'I've brought you a list of a kind,' said Mrs Oliver. 'I don't need to go into details of where I went or what I said or why, I went out deliberately for – well, information one couldn't perhaps get from anybody in this country now. But it's all from people who knew something about the Ravenscrofts, even if they hadn't known them very well.'

'News from foreign places, do you mean?'

'Quite a lot of them were from foreign places. Other people who knew them here rather slightly or from people whose aunts or cousins or friends knew them long ago.'

'And each one that you've noted down had *some* story to tell – some reference to the tragedy or to people involved?'

'That's the idea,' said Mrs Oliver. 'I'll tell you roughly, shall I?'

'Yes. Have a *petit-four*.'

'Thank you,' said Mrs Oliver.

She took a particularly sweet and rather bilious-looking one and champed it with energy.

'Sweet things,' she said, 'really give you a lot of vitality, I always think. Well now, I've got the following suggestions. These things have usually been said to me starting by: – "Oh yes, of course!" "How sad it was, that whole story!" "Of course, I think everyone knows really what happened." That's the sort of thing.'

'Yes.'

'These people *thought* they knew what happened. But there weren't really any very good reasons. It was just something someone had told them, or they'd heard either from friends or servants or relations or things like that. The suggestions, of course, are all the kind that you might think they were. A. That General Ravenscroft was writing his memoirs of his Malayan days and that he had a young woman who acted as his secretary and took dictation and typed things for him and was helping him, that she was a nice-looking girl and no doubt there was something there. The result being – well, there seemed to be two schools of thought. One school of thought was that he shot his wife because he hoped to marry the girl, and then when he had shot her, immediately was horror-stricken at what he'd done and shot himself . . .'

'Exactly,' said Poirot. 'A romantic explanation.'

'The other idea was that there had been a tutor who came to give lessons to the son who had been ill and away from his prep school for six months or so – a good-looking young man.'

'Ah yes. And the wife had fallen in love with the young man. Perhaps had an affair with him?'

'That was the idea,' said Mrs Oliver. 'No kind of evidence. Just romantic suggestion again.'

'And therefore?'

'Therefore I think the idea was that the General probably shot his wife and then in a fit of remorse shot himself. There was another story that the General had had an affair, and his wife found out about it, that she shot him and then herself. It's always been slightly different every time. But nobody really knew anything. I mean, it's always just a likely story every time. I mean, the General may have had an affair with a girl or lots of girls or just another married woman, or it might have been the wife who had an affair with someone. It's been a different someone in each story I've been told. There was nothing definite about it or any evidence for it. It's just the gossip that went around about twelve or thirteen years ago, which people have rather forgotten about now. But they remember enough about it to tell one a few names and get things only moderately wrong about what happened. There was an angry gardener who happened to live on the place, there was a nice elderly cook-housekeeper, who was rather blind and rather deaf, but nobody seems to suspect that she had anything to do with it.

And so on. I've got all the names and possibilities written down. The names of some of them wrong and some of them right. It's all very difficult. His wife had been ill, I gather, for some short time, I think it was some kind of fever that she had. A lot of her hair must have fallen out because she bought four wigs. There were at least four new wigs found among her things.'

'Yes. I, too, heard that,' said Poirot.

'Who did you hear it from?'

'A friend of mine in the police. He went back over the accounts of the inquest and the various things in the house. Four wigs! I would like to have your opinion on that, madame. Do you think that four wigs seems somewhat excessive?'

'Well, I do really,' said Mrs Oliver. 'I had an aunt who had a wig, and she had an extra wig, but she sent one back to be redressed and wore the second one. I never heard of anyone who had four wigs.'

Mrs Oliver extracted a small notebook from her bag, ruffled the pages of it, searching for extracts.

'Mrs Carstairs, she's seventy-seven and rather gaga. Quote from her: "I do remember the Ravenscrofts quite well. Yes, yes, a very nice couple. It's very sad, I think. Yes. Cancer it was!" I asked her which of them had cancer,' said Mrs Oliver, 'but Mrs Carstairs had rather forgotten about that. She said she thought the wife came to London and consulted a doctor and had an operation and then came home and was very miserable, and her husband was very upset about her. So of course he shot her and himself.'

'Was that her theory or did she have any exact knowledge?'

'I think it was entirely theory. As far as I can see and hear in the course of my investigations,' said Mrs Oliver, making rather a point of this last word, 'when anybody has heard that any of their friends whom they don't happen to know very well have sudden illnesses or consult doctors, they always think it's cancer. And so do the people themselves, I think. Somebody else – I can't read her name here, I've forgotten, I think it began with T – she said that it was the husband who had cancer. He was very unhappy, and so was his wife. And they talked it over together and they couldn't bear the thought of it all, so they decided to commit suicide.'

'Sad and romantic,' said Poirot.

'Yes, and I don't think really true,' said Mrs Oliver. 'It

is worrying, isn't it? I mean, the people remembering so much and that they really mostly seem to have made it up themselves.'

'They have made up the solution of something they knew about,' said Poirot. 'That is to say, they know that somebody comes to London, say, to consult a doctor, or that somebody has been in hospital for two or three months. That is a *fact* that they know.'

'Yes,' said Mrs Oliver, 'and then when they come to talk about it a long time afterwards, they've got the solution for it which they've made up themselves. That isn't awfully helpful, is it?'

'It is helpful,' said Poirot. 'You are quite right, you know, in what you said to me.'

'About elephants?' said Mrs Oliver, rather doubtfully.

'About elephants,' said Poirot. 'It is important to know certain facts which have lingered in people's memories although they may not know exactly what the fact was, why it happened or what led to it. But they might easily know something that we do not know and that we have no means of learning. So there have been memories leading to theories – theories of infidelity, of illness, of suicide pacts, of jealousy, all these things have been suggested to you. Further search could be made as to points if they seem in any way probable.'

'People like talking about the past,' said Mrs Oliver. 'They like talking about the past really much more than they like talking about what's happening now, or what happened last year. It brings things back to them. They tell you, of course, first about a lot of other people that you don't want to hear about and then you hear what the other people that they've remembered knew about somebody else that they didn't know but they heard about. You know, so that the General and Lady Ravenscroft you hear about is at one remove, as it were. It's like family relationships,' she said. 'You know, first cousin once removed, second cousin twice removed, all the rest of it. I don't think I've been really very helpful, though.'

'You must not think that,' said Poirot. 'I am pretty sure that you will find that some of these things in your agreeable little purple-coloured notebook will have something to do with the past tragedy. I can tell you from my own enquiries into the official accounts of these two deaths, that they have remained a mystery. That is, from the police point of view. They were an affectionate couple, there was no gossip or hearsay much about them of any sex trouble, there was no illness discovered such as would have caused anyone to take their own lives. I talk now only of the time, you understand, immediately preceding the tragedy. But there was a time before that, further back.'

'I know what you mean,' said Mrs Oliver, 'and I've got something about that from an old Nanny. An old Nanny who is now – I don't know, she might be a hundred, but I think she's only about eighty. I remember her from my childhood days. She used to tell me stories about people in the Services abroad – India, Egypt, Siam and Hong Kong and the rest.'

'Anything that interested you?'

'Yes,' said Mrs Oliver, 'there was some tragedy that she talked about. She seemed a bit uncertain about what it was. I'm not sure that it had anything to do with the Ravenscrofts, it might have been to do with some other people out there because she doesn't remember surnames and things very well. It was a mental case in one family. Someone's sister-in-law. Either General Whoever-it-was's sister or Mrs Whoever-it-was's sister. Somebody who'd been in a mental home for years. I gathered she'd killed her own children or tried to kill her own children long ago, and then she'd been supposed to be cured or paroled or something and came out to Egypt, or Malaya or wherever it was. She came out to stay with the people. And then it seems there was some other tragedy, connected again, I think, with children or something of that kind. Anyway, it was something that was hushed up. But I wondered. I mean, if there was something mental in the family, either Lady Ravenscroft's family or General Ravenscroft's family. I don't think it need have been as near as a sister. It could have been a cousin or something like that. But – well, it seemed to me a possible line of enquiry.'

'Yes,' said Poirot, 'there's always possibility and something that waits for many years and then comes home to roost from somewhere in the past. That is what someone said to me. *Old sins have long shadows.*'

'It seemed to me,' said Mrs Oliver, 'not that it was likely or even that old Nanny Matcham remembered it right or even really about it being the people she thought it was. But it *might* have fitted in with what that awful woman at the literary luncheon said to me.'

'You mean when she wanted to know . . .'

'Yes. When she wanted me to find out from the daughter,

my godchild, whether her mother had killed her father or whether her father had killed her mother.'

'And she thought the girl might know?'

'Well, it's likely enough that the girl would know. I mean, not at the time – it might have been shielded from her – but she might know things about it which would make her be aware what the circumstances were in their lives and who was likely to have killed whom, though she would probably never mention it or say anything about it or talk to anyone about it.'

'And you say that woman – this Mrs – '

'Yes. I've forgotten her name now. Mrs Burton some-thing. A name like that. She said something about her son had this girl-friend and that they were thinking of getting married. And I can quite see you might want to know, if so, whether her mother or father had criminal relations in their family – or a loony strain. She probably thought that if it was the mother who killed the father it would be very unwise for the boy to marry her, whereas if the father had killed the mother, she probably wouldn't mind as much,' said Mrs Oliver.

'You mean that she would think that the inheritance would go in the female line?'

'Well, she wasn't a very clever type of woman. Bossy,' said Mrs Oliver. 'Thinks she knows a lot, but no. I think you might think that way if you were a woman.'

'An interesting point of view, but possible,' said Poirot. 'Yes, I realize that.' He sighed. 'We have a lot to do still.'

'I've got another side light on things, too. Same thing, but second hand, if you know what I mean. You know. Someone says "The Ravenscrofts? Weren't they that couple who adopted a child? Then it seems, after it was all ar-ranged, and they were absolutely stuck on it – very, very keen on it, one of their children had died in Malaya, I think – but at any rate they had adopted this child and then its own mother wanted it back and they had a court case or something. But the court gave them the custody of the child and the mother came and tried to kidnap it back."'

'There are simpler points,' said Poirot, 'arising out of your report, points that I prefer.'

'Such as?'

'Wigs. Four wigs.'

'Well,' said Mrs Oliver, 'I thought that was interesting you but I don't know why. It doesn't seem to *mean* anything. The other story was just somebody mental. There are mental people who are in homes or loony-bins because they have killed their children or some other child, for some absolutely batty reason, no sense to it at all. I don't see why that would make General and Lady Ravenscroft want to kill themselves.'

'Unless one of them was implicated,' said Poirot.

'You mean that General Ravenscroft may have killed someone, a boy – an illegitimate child, perhaps, of his wife's or of his own? No, I think we're getting a bit too melodramatic there. Or she might have killed her husband's child or her own.'

'And yet,' said Poirot, 'what people seem to be, they usually are.'

'You mean – ?'

'They seemed an affectionate couple, a couple who lived together happily without disputes. They seem to have had no case history of illness beyond a suggestion of an operation, of someone coming to London to consult some medical authority, a possibility of cancer, of leukaemia, something of that kind, some future that they could not face. And yet, somehow we do not seem to get at something beyond what is *possible,* but not yet what is *probable.* If there was anyone else in the house, anyone else at the time, the police, my friends that is to say, who have known the investigation at the time, say that nothing told was really compatible with anything else but with the facts. For some reason, those two didn't want to go on living. *Why?*'

'I knew a couple,' said Mrs Oliver, 'in the war – the second war, I mean – they thought that the Germans would land in England and they had decided that if that happened they would kill themselves. I said it was very stupid. They said it would be impossible to go on living. It still seems to me stupid. You've got to have enough courage to live through something. I mean, it's not as though your death was going to do any good to anybody else. I wonder –'

'Yes, what do you wonder?'

'Well, when I said that I wondered suddenly if General and Lady Ravenscroft's deaths did any good to anyone else.'

'You mean somebody inherited money from them?'

'Yes. Not quite as blatant as that. Perhaps somebody would have a better chance of doing well in life. Something there was in their life that they didn't want either of their two children ever to hear about or to know about.'

Poirot sighed.

'The trouble with you, is,' he said, 'you think so often of something that well *might* have occurred, that *might* have been. You give me ideas. Possible ideas. If only they were probable ideas also. *Why*? Why were the deaths of those two necessary? Why is it – they were not in pain, they were not in illness, they were not deeply unhappy from what one can see. Then why, in the evening of a beautiful day, did they go for a walk to a cliff and taking the dog with them . . .'

'What's the dog got to do with it?' said Mrs Oliver.

'Well, I wondered for a moment. Did they take the dog, or did the dog follow them? Where does the dog come in?'

'I suppose it comes in like the wigs,' said Mrs Oliver. 'Just one more thing that you can't explain and doesn't seem to make sense. One of my elephants said the dog was devoted to Lady Ravenscroft, but another one said the dog bit her.'

'One always comes back to the same thing,' said Poirot. 'One wants to know more.' He sighed. 'One wants to know more about the people, and how can you know people separated from you by a gulf of years.'

'Well, you've done it once or twice, haven't you?' said Mrs Oliver. 'You know – something about where a painter was shot or poisoned. That was near the sea on a sort of fortification or something. You found out who did that, although you didn't know any of the people.'

'No. I didn't know any of the people, but I learnt about them from the other people who were there.'*

'Well, that's what I'm trying to do,' said Mrs Oliver, 'only I can't get near enough. I can't get to anyone who really knew anything, who was really involved. Do you think really we ought to give it up?'

'I think it would be very wise to give it up,' said Poirot, 'but there is a moment when one no longer wants to be wise. One wants to find out more. I have an interest now in that couple of kindly people, with two nice children. I presume they are nice children?'

'I don't know the boy,' said Mrs Oliver, 'I don't think I've ever met him. Do you want to see my goddaughter? I could send her to see you, if you like.'

* *Five Little Pigs*

'Yes, I think I would like to see her, meet her some way. Perhaps she would not wish to come and see me, but a meeting could be brought about. It might, I think, be interesting. And there is someone else I would like to see.'

'Oh! Who is that?'

'The woman at the party. The bossy woman. Your bossy friend.'

'She's no friend of mine,' said Mrs Oliver. 'She just came up and spoke to me, that's all.'

'You could resume acquaintance with her?'

'Oh yes, quite easily. I would think she'd probably jump at it.'

'I would like to see her. I would like to know why she wants to know these things.'

'Yes. I suppose that might be useful. Anyway –' Mrs Oliver sighed – 'I shall be glad to have a rest from elephants. Nanny – you know, the old Nanny I talked about – she mentioned elephants and that elephants didn't forget. That sort of silly sentence is beginning to haunt me. Ah well, *you* must look for more elephants. It's your turn.'

'And what about you?'

'Perhaps I could look for swans.'

'*Mon dieu*, where do swans come in?'

'It is only what I remember, which Nanny reminded me of. That there were little boys I used to play with and one used to call me Lady Elephant and the other one used to call me Lady Swan. When I was Lady Swan I pretended to be swimming about on the floor. When I was Lady Elephant they rode on my back. There are no swans in this.'

'That is a good thing,' said Poirot. 'Elephants are quite enough.'

Chapter 10

DESMOND

Two days later, as Hercule Poirot drank his morning chocolate, he read at the same time a letter that had been among his correspondence that morning. He was reading it now for the second time. The handwriting was a moderately good one, though it hardly bore the stamp of maturity.

Dear Monsieur Poirot,

I am afraid you will find this letter of mine somewhat peculiar, but I believe it would help if I mentioned a friend of yours. I tried to get in touch with her to ask her if she would arrange for me to come and see you, but apparently she had left home. Her secretary – I am referring to Mrs Ariadne Oliver, the novelist – her secretary seemed to say something about her having gone on a safari in East Africa. If so, I can see she may not return for some time. But I'm sure she would help me. I would indeed like to see you so much. I am badly in need of advice of some kind.

Mrs Oliver, I understand, is acquainted with my mother, who met her at a literary luncheon party. If you could give me an appointment to visit you one day I should be very grateful. I can suit my time to anything you suggested. I don't know if it is helpful at all but Mrs Oliver's secretary did mention the word 'elephants'. I presume this has something to do with Mrs Oliver's travels in East Africa. The secretary spoke as though it was some kind of pass-word. I don't really understand this but perhaps you will. I am in a great state of worry and anxiety and I would be very grateful if you could see me.

Yours truly,
Desmond Burton-Cox.

'*Nom d'un petit bonhomme!*' said Hercule Poirot.

'I beg your pardon, sir?' said George.

'A mere ejaculation,' said Hercule Poirot. 'There are some things, once they have invaded your life, which you find very difficult to get rid of again. With me it seems to be a question of elephants.'

He left the breakfast table, summoned his faithful secretary, Miss Lemon, handed her the letter from Desmond Cox and gave her directions to arrange an appointment with the writer of the letter.

'I am not too occupied at the present time,' he said. 'Tomorrow will be quite suitable.'

Miss Lemon reminded him of two appointments which he already had, but agreed that that left plenty of hours vacant and she would arrange something as he wished.

'Something to do with the Zoological Gardens?' she enquired.

'Hardly,' said Poirot. 'No, do not mention elephants in

your letter. There can be too much of anything. Elephants are large animals. They occupy a great deal of the horizon. Yes. We can leave elephants. They will no doubt arise in the course of the conversation I propose to hold with Desmond Burton-Cox.'

'Mr Desmond Burton-Cox,' announced George, ushering in the expected guest.

Poirot had risen to his feet and was standing beside the mantelpiece. He remained for a moment or two without speaking, then he advanced, having summed up his own impression. A somewhat nervous and energetic personality. Quite naturally so, Poirot thought. A little ill at ease but managing to mask it very successfully. He said, extending a hand,

'Mr Hercule Poirot?'

'That is right,' said Poirot. 'And your name is Desmond Burton-Cox. Pray sit down and tell me what I can do for you, the reasons why you have come to see me.'

'It's all going to be rather difficult to explain,' said Desmond Burton-Cox.

'So many things are difficult to explain,' said Hercule Poirot, 'but we have plenty of time. Sit down.'

Desmond looked rather doubtfully at the figure confronting him. Really, a very comic personality, he thought. The egg-shaped head, the big moustaches. Not somehow very imposing. Not quite, in fact, what he had expected to encounter.

'You – you are a detective, aren't you?' he said. 'I mean you – you find out things. People come to you to find out, or to ask you to find out things for them.'

'Yes,' said Poirot, 'that is one of my tasks in life.'

'I don't suppose that you know what I've come about or that you know anything much about me.'

'I know something,' said Poirot.'

'You mean Mrs Oliver, your friend Mrs Oliver. She's told you something?'

'She told me that she had had an interview with a goddaughter of hers, a Miss Celia Ravenscroft. That is right, is it not?'

'Yes. Yes, Celia told me. This Mrs Oliver, is she – does she also know my mother – know her well, I mean?'

'No. I do not think that they know each other well. According to Mrs Oliver, she met her at a literary luncheon recently and had a few words with her. Your mother, I understand, made a certain request to Mrs Oliver.'

'She'd no business to do so,' said the boy.

His eyebrows came down over his nose. He looked angry now, angry – almost revengeful.

'Really,' he said, 'Mothers – I mean – '

'I understand,' said Poirot. 'There is much feeling these days, indeed perhaps there always has been. Mothers are continually doing things which their children would much rather they did not. Am I right?'

'Oh you're right enough. But my mother – I mean, she interferes in things in which really she has no concern.'

'You and Celia Ravenscroft, I understand, are close friends. Mrs Oliver understood from your mother that there was some question of marriage. Perhaps in the near future?'

'Yes, but my mother really doesn't need to ask questions and worry about things which are – well, no concern of hers.'

'But mothers are like that,' said Poirot. He smiled faintly. He added, 'You are, perhaps, very much attached to your mother?'

'I wouldn't say that,' said Desmond. 'No, I certainly wouldn't say that. You see – well, I'd better tell you straight away, she's not really my mother.'

'Oh, indeed. I had not understood that.'

'I'm adopted,' said Desmond. 'She had a son. A little boy who died. And then she wanted to adopt a child so I was adopted, and she brought me up as her son. She always speaks of me as her son, and thinks of me as her son, but I'm not really. We're not a bit alike. We don't look at things the same way.'

'Very understandable,' said Poirot.

'I don't seem to be getting on,' said Desmond, 'with what I want to ask you.'

'You want me to do something, to find out something, to cover a certain line of interrogation?'

'I suppose that does cover it. I don't know how much you know about – about well, what the trouble is all about.'

'I know a little,' said Poirot. 'Not details. I do not know very much about you or about Miss Ravenscroft, whom I have not yet met. I'd like to meet her.'

'Yes, well, I was thinking of bringing her to talk to you but I thought I'd better talk to you myself first.'

'Well, that seems quite sensible,' said Poirot. 'You are

unhappy about something? Worried? You have difficulties?'

'Not really. No. No, there shouldn't be any difficulties. There aren't any. What happened is a thing that happened years ago when Celia was only a child, or a schoolgirl at least. And there was a tragedy, the sort of thing that happens – well, it happens every day, any time. Two people you know whom something has upset very much and they commit suicide. A sort of suicide pact, this was. Nobody knew very much about it or why, or anything like that. But, after all, it happens and it's no business really of people's children to worry about it. I mean, if they know the facts that's quite enough, I should think. And it's no business of my mother's *at all.*'

'As one journeys through life,' said Poirot, 'one finds more and more that people are often interested in things that are none of their own business. Even more so than they are in things that *could* be considered as their own business.'

'But this is all over. Nobody knew much about it or anything. But, you see, my mother keeps asking questions. Wants to know things, and she's got at Celia. She's got Celia into a state where she doesn't really know whether she wants to marry me or not.'

'And you? You know if you want to marry her still?'

'Yes, of course I know. I mean to marry her. I'm quite determined to marry her. But she's got upset. She wants to know things. She wants to know why all this happened and she thinks – I'm sure she's wrong – she thinks that my mother knows something about it. That she's heard something about it.'

'Well, I have much sympathy for you,' said Poirot, 'but it seems to me that if you are sensible young people and if you want to marry, there is no reason why you should not. I may say that I have been given some information at my request about this sad tragedy. As you say, it is a matter that happened years ago. There was no full explanation of it. There never has been. But in life one cannot have explanations of all the sad things that happen.'

'It was a suicide pact,' said the boy. 'It couldn't have been anything else. But – well . . .'

'You want to know the cause of it. Is that it?'

'Well, yes, that's it. That's what Celia's been worried about, and she's almost made me worried. Certainly my mother is worried, though, as I've said, it's absolutely no business of hers. I don't think any fault is attached to anyone. I mean, there wasn't a row or anything. The trouble is, of course, that we don't know. Well, I mean, I shouldn't know anyway because I wasn't there.'

'You didn't know General and Lady Ravenscroft or Celia?'

'I've known Celia more or less all my life. You see, the people I went to for holidays and her people lived next door to each other when we were very young. You know – just children. And we always liked each other, and got on together and all that. And then of course, for a long time all that passed over. I didn't meet Celia for a great many years after that. Her parents, you see, were in Malaya, and so were mine. I think they met each other again there – I mean my father and mother. My father's dead, by the way. But I think when my mother was in Malaya she heard things and she's remembered now what she heard and she's worked herself up about them and she sort of – sort of thinks things that can't possibly be true. I'm sure they aren't true. But she's determined to worry Celia about them. I want to know what really happened. Celia wants to know what really happened. What it was all about. And why? And how? Not just people's silly stories.'

'Yes,' said Poirot, 'it is not unnatural perhaps that you should both feel that. Celia, I should imagine, more than you. She is more disturbed by it than you are. But, if I may say so, does it really matter? What matters is the *now*, the *present*. The girl you want to marry, the girl who wants to marry you – what has the past to do with you? Does it matter whether her parents had a suicide pact or whether they died in an aeroplane accident or one of them was killed in an accident and the other one later committed suicide? Whether there were love-affairs which came into their lives and made for unhappiness.'

'Yes,' said Desmond Burton-Cox, 'yes, I think what you say is sensible and quite right but – well, things have been built up in such a way that I've got to make sure that Celia is satisfied. She's – she's a person who *minds* about things although she doesn't talk about them much.'

'Has it not occurred to you,' said Hercule Poirot, 'that it may be very difficult, if not impossible, to find out what really happened.'

'You mean which of them killed the other or why, or that one shot the other and then himself. Not unless – not unless there had been *something*.'

'Yes, but that something would have been in the past,

so why does it matter now?'

'It oughtn't to matter – it wouldn't matter but for my mother interfering, poking about in things. It wouldn't have mattered. I don't suppose that, well, Celia's ever thought much about it. I think probably that she was away at school in Switzerland at the time the tragedy happened and nobody told her much and, well, when you're a teenager or younger still you just accept things as something that happened, but that's not anything to do with you really.'

'Then don't you think that perhaps you're wanting the impossible?'

'I want you to find out,' said Desmond. 'Perhaps it's not the kind of thing that you can find out, or that you like finding out – '

'I have no objection to finding out,' said Poirot. 'In fact one has even a certain – curiosity, shall I say. Tragedies, things that arise as a matter of grief, surprise, shock, illness, they are human tragedies, human things, and it is only natural that if one's attention is drawn to them one should want to know. What I say is, is it wise or necessary to rake up things?'

'Perhaps it isn't,' said Desmond, 'but you see . . .'

'And also,' said Poirot, interrupting him, 'don't you agree with me that it is rather an impossible thing to do after all this time?'

'No,' said Desmond, 'that's where I *don't* agree with you. I think it would be quite possible.'

'Very interesting,' said Poirot. 'Why do you think it would be quite possible?'

'Because – '

'Of what? You have a reason.'

'I think there are people who would know. I think there are people who *could* tell you if they were willing to tell you. People, perhaps, who would not wish to tell me, who would not wish to tell Celia, but *you* might find out from them.'

'That is interesting,' said Poirot.

'Things happened,' said Desmond. 'Things happened in the past. I – I've sort of heard about them in a vague way. There was some mental trouble. There was someone – I don't know who exactly, I think it might have been Lady Ravenscroft – I think she was in a mental home for years. Quite a long time. Some tragedy had happened when she was quite young. Some child who died or an accident. Something that – well, she was concerned in it in some way.'

'It is not what you know of your own knowledge, I presume?'

'No. It's something my mother said. Something she heard. She heard it in Malaya, I think. Gossip there from other people. You know how they get together in the Services, people like that, and the women all gossip together – all the memsahibs. Saying things that mightn't be true at all.'

'And you want to know whether they were true or were not true?'

'Yes, and I don't know how to find out myself. Not now, because it was a long time ago and I don't know who to ask. I don't know who to go to, but until we really find out what did happen and why –'

'What you mean is,' said Poirot, 'at least I think I am right only this is pure surmise on my part, Celia Ravenscroft does not want to marry you unless she is quite sure that there is no mental flaw passed to her presumably by her mother. Is that it?'

'I think that is what she has got into her head somehow. And I think my mother put it there. I think it's what my mother wants to believe. I don't think she's any reason really for believing it except ill-mannered spite and gossip and all the rest of it.'

'It will not be a very easy thing to investigate,' said Poirot.

'No, but I've heard things about you. They say that you're very clever at finding out what did happen. Asking people questions and getting them to tell you things.'

'Whom do you suggest I should question or ask? When you say Malaya, I presume you are not referring to people of Malayan nationality. You are speaking of what you might call the memsahib days, the days when there were Service communities in Malaya. You are speaking of English people and the gossip in some English station there.'

'I don't really mean that that would be any good now. I think whoever it was who gossiped, who talked – I mean, it's so long ago now that they'd have forgotten all about it, that they are probably dead themselves. I think that my mother's got a lot of things wrong, that she's heard things and made up more things about them in her mind.'

'And you still think that I would be capable –'

'Well, I don't mean that I want you to go out to Malaya and ask people things. I mean, none of the people would be there now.'

'So you think you could not give me names?'

'Not those sort of names,' said Desmond.

'But some names?'

'Well, I'll come out with what I mean. I think there are two people who might know what happened and why. Because, you see, they'd have been *there*. They'd have *known*, really known, of their own knowledge.'

'You do not want to go to them yourself?'

'Well, I could. I have in a way, but I don't think, you see, that they – I don't know. I wouldn't like to ask some of the things I want to ask. I don't think Celia would. They're very nice, and that's *why* they'd know. Not because they're nasty, not because they gossip, but because they might have helped. They might have done something to make things better, or have tried to do so, only they couldn't. Oh, I'm putting it all so badly.'

'No,' said Poirot, 'you are doing it very well, and I am interested and I think you have something definite in your mind. Tell me, does Celia Ravenscroft agree with you?'

'I haven't said too much to her. You see, she was very fond of Maddy and of Zélie.'

'Maddy and Zélie?'

'Oh well, that's their names. Oh, I must explain. I haven't done it very well. You see, when Celia was quite a child – at the time when I first knew her, as I say, when we were living next door in the country – she had a French sort of – well, I suppose nowadays we call it an *au pair* girl but it was called a governess then. You know, a French governess. A mademoiselle. And you see, she was very nice. She played with all of us children and Celia always called her "Maddy" for short – and all the family called her Maddy.'

'Ah yes. The mademoiselle.'

'Yes, you see being French I thought – I thought perhaps she would tell you things that she knew and wouldn't wish to speak about to other people.'

'Ah. And the other name you mentioned?'

'Zélie. The same sort of thing, you see. A mademoiselle. Maddy was there, I think, for about two or three years and then, later, she went back to France, or Switzerland I think it was, and this other one came. Younger than Maddy was and we didn't call her Maddy. Celia called her Zélie. All the family called her Zélie. She was very young, pretty and great fun. We were all frightfully fond of her. She played games with us and we all loved her. The family did. And General Ravenscroft was very taken with her. They used to play games together, picquet, you know and lots of things.'

'And Lady Ravenscroft?'

'Oh she was devoted to Zélie too, and Zélie was devoted to her. That's why she came back again after she'd left.'

'Came back?'

'Yes, when Lady Ravenscroft was ill, and had been in hospital, Zélie came back and was sort of companion to her and looked after her. I don't know, but I believe, I think, I'm almost sure that she was there when it – the tragedy – happened. And so, you see she'd *know* – what really happened.'

'And you know her address? You know where she is now?'

'Yes. I know where she is. I've got her address. I've got both their addresses. I thought perhaps you could go and see her, or both of them. I know it's a lot to ask – ' He broke off.

Poirot looked at him for some minutes. Then he said: 'Yes, it is a possibility – certainly – a possibility.'

BOOK 2

Long Shadows

Chapter 11

SUPERINTENDENT GARROWAY AND POIROT COMPARE NOTES

Superintendent Garroway looked across the table at Poirot. His eyes twinkled. At his side George delivered a whisky and soda. Passing on to Poirot, he put down a glass filled with a dark purple liquid.

'What's your tipple?' said Superintendent Garroway, with some interest.

'A syrup of black currant,' said Poirot.

'Well, well,' said Superintendent Garroway, 'everyone to their own taste. What was it Spence told me? He told me you used to drink something called a tisane, wasn't it? What's that, a variant of French piano or something?'

'No,' said Poirot, 'it's useful for reducing fevers.'

'Ah. Invalid dope of some kind.' He drank from his glass. 'Well,' he said, 'here's to suicide!'

'It *was* suicide?' Poirot asked.

'What else can it be?' said Superintendent Garroway. 'The things you wanted to know!' He shook his head. His smile grew more pronounced.

'I am sorry,' said Poirot, 'to have troubled you so much. I am like the animal or the child in one of your stories by Mr Kipling. I Suffer from Insatiable Curiosity.'

'Insatiable curiosity,' said Superintendent Garroway. 'Nice stories he wrote, Kipling. Knew his stuff, too. They told me once that that man could go for one short tour round a destroyer and know more about it than one of the top engineers in the Royal Navy.'

'Alas,' said Hercule Poirot, 'I do not know everything. Therefore, you see, I have to ask questions. I am afraid that I sent you rather a long list of questions.'

'What intrigued me,' said Superintendent Garroway, 'is

the way you jumped from one thing to another. Psychiatrists, doctors' reports, how money was left, who had money, who got money. Who expected money and didn't get money, particulars of ladies' hairdressing, wigs, name of the supplier of wigs, charming rose-coloured cardboard boxes they came in by the way.'

'You knew all these things,' said Poirot. 'That has amazed me, I can assure you.'

'Ah well, it was a puzzling case and of course we made full notes on the subject. None of this was any good to us but we kept the files and it was all there if one wanted to look for it.'

He pushed a piece of paper across the table.

'Here you are. Hairdressers. Bond Street. Expensive firm. Eugene and Rosentelle was the name of it. They moved later. Same firm but went into business in Sloane Street. Here's the address, but it's a Pet Shop now. Two of their assistants retired some years ago now, but they were the top assistants serving people then, and Lady Ravenscroft was on their list. Rosentelle lives in Cheltenham now. Still in the same line of business – Calls herself a Hair Stylist – That's the up-to-date term – and you add Beautician. Same man, different hat, as one used to say in my young days.'

'Ah-ha?' said Poirot.

'Why ah-ha?' asked Garroway.

'I am immensely obliged to you,' said Hercule Poirot. 'You have presented me with an idea. How strange it is the way ideas arrive into one's head.'

'You've too many ideas in your head already,' said the Superintendent, 'that's one of your troubles – you don't need any more. Now then, I've checked up as well as I could on the family history – nothing much there. Alistair Ravenscroft was of Scottish extraction. Father was a clergyman – two uncles in the Army – both quite distinguished. Married Margaret Preston-Grey – well-born girl – presented at Court and all the rest of it. No family scandals. You were quite right about her being one of twin sisters. Don't know where you picked that up – Dorothea and Margaret Preston-Grey – known colloquially as Dolly and Molly. The Preston-Greys lived at Hatters Green in Sussex. Identical twins – usual kind of history of that kind of twin. Cut their first tooth the same day – both got scarlet fever the same month – wore the same kind of clothes – fell in love with the same kind of man – got married about the same time – both husbands in the

Army. Family doctor who attended the family when they were young died some years ago, so there's nothing of interest to be got out of him. There was an early tragedy, though, connected with one of them.'

'Lady Ravenscroft?'

'No, the other one – she married a Captain Jarrow – had two children; the younger one, a boy of four, was knocked down by a wheelbarrow or some kind of child's garden toy – or a spade or a child's hoe. Hit him on his head and he fell into an artificial pond or something and drowned. Apparently it was the older child, a girl of nine who did it. They were playing together and quarrelled, as children do. Doesn't seem much doubt, but there *was* another story. Someone said the mother did it – got angry and hit him – and someone else said it was a woman who lived next door who hit him. Don't suppose it's of any interest to you – no bearing on a suicide pact entered into by the mother's sister and her husband years after.'

'No,' said Poirot, 'it does not seem to. But one likes to know background.'

'Yes,' said Garroway, 'as I told you, one has to look into the past. I can't say we'd thought of looking into the past as long ago as this. I mean, as I've said, all this was some years before the suicide.'

'Were there any proceedings at the time?'

'Yes. I managed to look up the case. Accounts of it. Newspaper accounts. Various things. There were some doubts about it, you know. The mother was badly affected. She broke down completely and had to go into hospital. They do say she was never the same woman again afterwards.'

'But they thought she had done it?'

'Well, that's what the doctor thought. There was no direct evidence, you understand. She said that she had seen this happen from a window, that she'd seen the older child, the girl, hit the boy and push him in. But her account – well, I don't think they believed it at the time. She talked so wildly.'

'There was, I suppose, some psychiatric evidence?'

'Yes. She went to a nursing home or hospital of some kind, she was definitely a mental case. She was a good long time in one or two different establishments having treatment, I believe under the care of one of the specialists from St Andrew's Hospital in London. In the end she was pronounced cured, and released after about three years,

100

and sent home to lead a normal life with her family.'

'And she was then quite normal?'

'She was always neurotic, I believe – '

'Where was she at the time of the suicide? Was she staying with the Ravenscrofts?'

'No – she had died nearly three weeks before that. She was staying with them at Overcliffe when it happened. It seemed again to be an illustration of the identical twin destiny. She walked in her sleep – had suffered from that over a period of years, it seems. She had had one or two minor accidents that way. Sometimes she took too many tranquillizers and that resulted in her walking round the house and sometimes out of it during the night. She was following a path along the cliff edge, lost her footing and fell over the cliff. Killed immediately – they didn't find her until the next day. Her sister, Lady Ravenscroft, was terribly upset. They were very devoted to each other and she had to be taken to hospital suffering from shock.'

'Could this tragic accident have led to the Ravenscrofts' suicide some weeks later?'

'There was never a suggestion of such a thing.'

'Odd things happen with twins as you say – Lady Ravenscroft might have killed herself because of the link between her and her twin sister. Then the husband may have shot himself because possibly he felt guilty in some way – '

Superintendent Garroway said: 'You have too many ideas, Poirot. Alistair Ravenscroft couldn't have had an affair with his sister-in-law without everyone knowing about it. There was nothing of that kind – if that's what you've been imagining.'

The telephone rang – Poirot rose and answered it. It was Mrs Oliver.

'Monsieur Poirot, can you come to tea or sherry tomorrow? I have got Celia coming – and later on the bossy woman. That's what you wanted, isn't it?'

Poirot said it was just what he wanted.

'I've got to dash now,' said Mrs Oliver, 'Going to meet an old War Horse – provided by my elephant No. 1, Julia Carstairs. I think she's got his name wrong – she always does – but I hope she's got his address right.'

Chapter 12

CELIA MEETS HERCULE POIROT

'Well, madame,' said Poirot, 'and how did you fare with Sir Hugo Foster?'

'To begin with his name wasn't Foster – it was Fothergill. Trust Julia to get a name wrong. She's always doing it.'

'So elephants are not always reliable in the names they remember?'

'Don't talk of elephants – I've finished with elephants.'

'And your War Horse?'

'Quite an old pet – but useless as a source of information. Obsessed by some people called Barnet who did have a child killed in an accident in Malaya. But nothing to do with the Ravenscrofts. I tell you I've finished with elephants –'

'Madame, you have been most persevering, most noble.'

'Celia is coming along in about half an hour's time. You wanted to meet her, didn't you? I've told her that you are – well, helping me in this matter. Or would you rather she came to see you?'

'No,' said Poirot, 'I think I should like her to come in the way you have arranged.'

'I don't suppose she'll stay very long. If we get rid of her in about an hour, that would be all right, just to think over things a bit, and then Mrs Burton-Cox is coming.'

'Ah yes. That will be interesting. Yes, that will be very interesting.'

Mrs Oliver sighed. 'Oh dear, it's a pity, though, isn't it?' She said again, 'We do have too much material, don't we?'

'Yes,' said Poirot. 'We do not know what we are looking for. All we know of still is, in all probability, the double suicide of a married couple who lived quiet and happy lives together. And what have we got to show for cause, for reason? We've gone forward and back to the right, to the left, to the west, to the east.'

'Quite right,' said Mrs Oliver. 'Everywhere. We haven't

been to the North Pole yet,' she added.

'Nor to the South Pole,' said Poirot.

'So what is there, when it all comes to it?'

'Various things,' said Poirot. 'I have made here a list. Do you want to read it?'

Mrs Oliver came over and sat beside him and looked over his shoulder.

'Wigs,' she said, pointing to the first item. 'Why wigs first?'

'Four wigs,' said Poirot, 'seem to be interesting. Interesting and rather difficult to solve.'

'I believe the shop she got her wigs from has gone out of the trade now. People go to quite different places for wigs and they're not wearing so many as they did just then. People used to wear wigs to go abroad. You know, because it saves bother in travelling.'

'Yes, yes,' said Poirot, 'we will do what we can with wigs. Anyway, that is one thing that interests me. And then there are other stories. Stories of mental disturbance in the family. Stories of a twin sister who was mentally disturbed and spent a good many years of her life in a mental home.'

'It doesn't seem to lead anywhere,' said Mrs Oliver. 'I mean to say, I suppose she could have come and shot the two of them, but I don't really see why.'

'No,' said Poirot, 'the fingerprints on the revolver were definitely only the fingerprints of General Ravenscroft and his wife, I understand. Then there are stories of a child, a child in Malaya was murdered or attacked, possibly by this twin sister of Lady Ravenscroft. Possibly by some quite different woman – possibly by an amah or a servant. Point two. You know a little more about money.'

'Where does money come into it?' said Mrs Oliver, in some surprise.

'It does not come into it,' said Poirot. 'That is what is so interesting. Money usually comes in. Money someone got as a result of that suicide. Money lost as a result of it. Money somewhere causing difficulties, causing trouble, causing covetousness and desire. It is difficult, that. Difficult to see. There does not seem to have been any large amount of money anywhere. There are various stories of love-affairs, women who were attractive to the husband, men who were attractive to the wife. An affair on one side or the other could have led to suicide or to murder. It very often does. Then we come to what at the moment inclines me to the most interest. That is why I am so anxious to meet Mrs Burton-Cox.'

'Oh. That awful woman. I don't see why you think she's important. All she did was to be a noseyparker and want me to find out things.'

'Yes, but why did she want you to find out things? It seems to me very odd, that. It seems to me that that is something that one has to find out about. She is the link, you see.'

'The link?'

'Yes. We do not know what the link was, where it was, how it was. All we know is that she wants desperately to learn more about this suicide. Being a link, she connects both with your godchild, Celia Ravenscroft, and with the son who is not her son.'

'What do you mean – not her son?'

'He is an adopted son,' said Poirot. 'A son she adopted because her own son died.'

'How did her own child die? Why? When?'

'All these things I asked myself. She could be a link, a link of emotion, a wish for revenge through hatred, through some love-affair. At any rate I must see her. I must make up my mind about her. Yes. I cannot help but think that is very important.'

There was a ring at the bell and Mrs Oliver went out of the room to answer it.

'This, I think, could be Celia,' she said. 'You're sure it's all right?'

'By me, yes,' said Poirot. 'By her also, I hope.'

Mrs Oliver came back a few minutes later. Celia Ravenscroft was with her. She had a doubtful, suspicious look.

'I don't know,' she said, 'if I –' She stopped, staring at Hercule Poirot.

'I want to introduce you,' said Mrs Oliver, 'to someone who is helping me, and I hope is helping you also. That is, helping you in what you want to know and to find out. This is Monsieur Hercule Poirot. He has special genius in finding out things.'

'Oh,' said Celia.

She looked very doubtfully at the egg-shaped head, the monstrous moustaches and the small stature.

'I think,' she said, rather doubtfully, 'that I have heard of him.'

Hercule Poirot stopped himself with a slight effort from saying firmly 'Most people have heard of me.' It was not quite as true as it used to be because many people who had heard of Hercule Poirot and known him, were now reposing with suitable memorial stones over them, in churchyards. He said,

'Sit down, mademoiselle. I will tell you this much about myself. That when I start an investigation I pursue it to the end. I will bring to light the truth and if it is, shall we say, truly the truth that you want, then I will deliver that knowledge to you. But it may be that you want reassuring. That is not the same thing as the truth. I can find various aspects that might reassure you. Will that be enough? If so, do not ask for more.'

Celia sat down in the chair he had pushed towards her, and looked at him rather earnestly. Then she said,

'You don't think I'd care for the truth, is that it?'

'I think,' said Poirot, 'that the truth might be – a shock,. a sorrow, and it might be that you would have said "why did I not leave all this behind? Why did I ask for knowledge? It is painful knowledge about which I can do nothing helpful or hopeful." It is a double suicide by a father and a mother that I – well, we'll admit it – that I loved. It is not a disadvantage to love a mother and father.'

'It seems to be considered so nowadays occasionally,' said Mrs Oliver. 'New article of belief, shall we say.'

'That's the way I've been living,' said Celia. 'Beginning to wonder, you know. Catching on to odd things that people said sometimes. People who looked at me rather pityingly. But more than that. With curiosity as well. One begins to find out, you know, things about people, I mean. People you meet, people you know, people who used to know your family. I don't want this life. I want . . . you think I don't really want it but I do – I want truth. I'm able to deal with truth. Just tell me something.'

It was not a continuation of the conversation. Celia had turned on Poirot with a separate question. Something which had replaced what had been in her mind just previously.

'You saw Desmond, didn't you?' she said. 'He went to see you. He told me he had.'

'Yes. He came to see me. Did you not want him to do so?'

'He didn't ask me.'

'If he had asked you?'

'I don't know. I don't know whether I should have forbidden him to do so, told him on no account to do such a thing, or whether I should have encouraged it.'

'I would like to ask you one question, mademoiselle. I want to know if there is one clear thing in your mind that matters to you, that could matter to you more than anythings else.'

'Well, what is that?'

'As you say, Desmond Burton-Cox came to see me. A very atractive and likeable young man, and very much in earnest over what he came to say. Now that – that is the really important thing. The important thing is if you and he really wish to marry – because that *is* serious. That is – though young people do not always think so nowadays – that is a link together for life. Do you want to enter into that state? It matters. What difference can it make to you or to Desmond whether the death of two people was a double suicide or something quite different?'

'You think it *is* something quite different – or, it was?'

'I do not as yet know,' said Poirot. 'I have reason to believe that it might be. There are certain things that do not accord with a double suicide, but as far as I can go on the opinion of the police – and the police are very reliable, Mademoiselle Celia, very reliable – they put together all the evidence and they thought very definitely that it could be nothing else but a double suicide.'

'But they never knew the cause of it? That's what you mean.'

'Yes,' said Poirot, 'that's what I mean.'

'And don't you know the cause of it, either? I mean, from looking into things or thinking about them, or whatever you do?'

'No, I am not sure about it,' said Poirot. 'I think there might be something very painful to learn and I am asking you whether you will be wise enough to say: "The past is the past. Here is a young man whom I care for and who cares for me. This is the future we are spending together, not the past." '

'Did he tell you he was an adopted child?' asked Celia.

'Yes, he did.'

'You see, what business is it really, of hers? Why should she come worrying Mrs Oliver here, trying to make Mrs

Oliver ask me questions, find out things? She's not his own mother.'

'Does he care for her?'

'No,' said Celia. 'I'd say on the whole he dislikes her. I think he always has.'

'She's spent money on him, schooling and on clothes and on all sorts of different things. And you think *she* cares for *him*?'

'I don't know. I don't think so. She wanted, I suppose, a child to replace her own child. She'd had a child who died in an accident, that was why she wanted to adopt someone, and her husband had died quite recently. All these dates are so difficult.'

'I know, I know. I would like perhaps to know one thing.'

'About her or about him?'

'Is he provided for financially?'

'I don't know quite what you mean by that. He'll be able to support me – to support a wife. I gather some money was settled on him when he was adopted. A sufficient sum, that is. I don't mean a fortune or anything like that.'

'There is nothing that she could – withhold?'

'What, you mean that she'd cut off the money supplies if he married me? I don't think she's ever threatened to do that, or indeed that she could do it. I think it was all fixed up by lawyers or whoever arranges adoptions. I mean, they make a lot of fuss, these adoption societies, from all I hear.'

'I would ask you something else which you might know but nobody else does. Presumably Mrs Burton-Cox knows it. Do you know who his actual mother was?'

'You think that might have been one of the reasons for her being so nosey and all that? Something to do with, as you say, what he was really. I don't know. I suppose he might have been an illegitimate child. They're the usual ones that go for adoption, aren't they? She might have known something about his real mother or his real father, or something like that. If so, she didn't tell him. I gather she just told him the silly things they suggest you should say. That it is just as nice to be adopted because it shows you really were wanted. There's a lot of silly slop like that.'

'I think some societies suggest that that's the way you should break the news. Does he or you know of any blood relations?'

'I don't know. I don't think he knows, but I don't think it worries him at all. He's not that kind of a worrier.'

'Do you know if Mrs Burton-Cox was a friend of your family, of your mother and father? Did you ever meet her as far as you can remember, when you were living in your own home in the early days?'

'I don't think so. I think Desmond's mother – I mean, I think Mrs Burton-Cox went to Malaya. I think perhaps her husband died out in Malaya, and that Desmond was sent to school in England while they were out there and that he was boarded with some cousins or people who take in children for holidays. And that's how we came to be friends in those days. I always remembered him, you know. I was a great hero-worshipper. He was wonderful at climbing trees and he taught me things about birds' nests and birds' eggs. So it seemed quite natural, when I met him again I mean, met him at the university, and we both talked about where we'd lived and then he asked me my name. He said "Only your Christian name I know," and then we remembered quite a lot of things together. It's what made us, you might say, get acquainted. I don't know everything about him. I don't know *anything*. I want to know. How can you arrange your life and know what you're going to do with your life if you don't know all about the things that affect you, that really happened?'

'So you tell me to carry on with my investigation?'

'Yes, if it's going to produce any results, though I don't think it will be because in a way, well, Desmond and I have tried our hand at finding out a few things. We haven't been very successful. It seems to come back to this plain fact which isn't really the story of a life. It's the story of a death, isn't it? Of two deaths, that's to say. When it's a double suicide, one thinks of it as one death. Is it in Shakespeare or where does the quotation come from – "And in death they were not divided." ' She turned to Poirot again. 'Yes, go on. Go on finding out. Go on telling Mrs Oliver or telling me direct. I'd rather you told me direct.' She turned towards Mrs Oliver. 'I don't mean to be horrid to you, Godmother. You've been a very nice godmother to me always, but – but I'd like it straight from the horse's mouth. I'm afraid that's rather rude, Monsieur Poirot, but I didn't mean it that way.'

'No,' said Poirot, 'I am content to be the horse's mouth.'

'And you think you will be?'

'I always believe that I can.'

'And it's always true, is it?'

'It is usually true,' said Poirot. 'I do not say more than that.'

Chapter 13

MRS BURTON-COX

'Well,' said Mrs Oliver as she returned into the room after seeing Celia to the door. 'What do you think of her?'

'She is a personality,' said Poirot, 'an interesting girl. Definitely, if I may put it so, she is somebody, not anybody.'

'Yes, that's true enough,' said Mrs Oliver.

'I would like you to tell me something.'

'About her? I don't really know her very well. One doesn't really, with godchildren. I mean, you only see them, as it were, at stated intervals rather far apart.'

'I didn't mean her. Tell me about her mother.'

'Oh. I see.'

'You knew her mother?'

'Yes. We were in a sort of *pensionnat* in Paris together. People used to send girls to Paris then to be finished,' said Mrs Oliver. 'That sounds more like an introduction to a cemetery than an introduction into Society. What do you want to know about her?'

'You remember her? You remember what she was like?'

'Yes. As I tell you, one doesn't entirely forget things or people because they're in the past.'

'What impression did she make on you?'

'She was beautiful,' said Mrs Oliver. 'I do remember that. Not when she was about thirteen or fourteen. She had a lot of puppy fat then. I think we all did,' she added, thoughtfully.

'Was she a personality?'

'It's difficult to remember because, you see, she wasn't my only friend or my greatest friend. I mean, there were several of us together – a little pack, as you might say. People with tastes more or less the same. We were keen on tennis and we were keen on being taken to the opera and

109

we were bored to death being taken to the picture galleries.
I really can only give you a general idea.

'Molly Preston-Grey. That was her name.'

'You both had boy-friends?'

'We had one or two passions, I think. Not for pop
singers, of course. They hadn't happened yet. Actors usually.
There was one rather famous variety actor. A girl – one
of the girls – had him pinned up over her bed and Mademoiselle Girand, the French mistress, on no account allowed that
actor to be pinned up there. "*Ce n'est pas convenable*," she
said. The girl didn't tell her that he was her father! We
laughed,' added Mrs Oliver. 'Yes, we laughed a good deal.'

'Well, tell me more about Molly or Margaret Preston-
Grey. Does this girl remind you of her?'

'No, I don't think she does. No. They are not alike. I
think Molly was more – was more emotional than this girl.'

'There was a twin sister, I understand. Was she at the
same *pensionnat*?'

'No, she wasn't. She might have been since they were
the same age, but no, I think she was in some entirely
different place in England. I'm not sure. I have a feeling
that the twin sister Dolly, whom I had met once or twice
very occasionally and who of course at that time looked
exactly like Molly – I mean they hadn't started trying to
look different, have different hair-dos and all that, as twins
do usually when they grow up. I think Molly was devoted
to her sister Dolly, but she didn't talk about her very much.
I have a feeling – nowadays, I mean, I didn't have it then –
that there might have been something a bit wrong perhaps
with the sister even then. Once or twice, I remember, there
were mentions of her having been ill or gone away for a
course of treatment somewhere. Something like that. I remember once wondering whether she was a cripple. She
was taken once by an aunt on a sea voyage to do her health
good.' She shook her head. 'I can't really remember, though.
I just had a feeling that Molly was devoted to her and
would have liked to have protected her in some way. Does
that seem nonsense to you?'

'Not at all,' said Hercule Poirot.

'There were other times, I think, when she didn't want
to talk about her. She talked about her mother and her
father. She was fond of them, I think, in the ordinary
sort of way. Her mother came once to Paris and took her
out, I remember. Nice woman. Not very exciting or good-

looking or anything. Nice, quiet, kindly.'

'I see. So you have nothing to help us there? No boy-friends?'

'We didn't have so many boy-friends then,' said Mrs Oliver. 'It's not like nowadays when it's a matter of course. Later, when we were both back again at home we more or less drifted apart. I think Molly went abroad somewhere with her parents. I don't think it was India – I don't think so. Somewhere else I think it was. Egypt perhaps. I think now they were in the Diplomatic Service. They were in Sweden at one time, and after that somewhere like Bermuda or the West Indies. I think he was a Governor or something there. But those sort of things one doesn't really remember. All one remembers is all the silly things that we said to each other. I had a crush on the violin master, I remember. Molly was very keen on the music master, which was very satisfying to us both and I should think much less troublesome than boy-friends seem to be nowadays. I mean, you adored – longed for the day when they came again to teach you. They were, I have no doubt, quite indifferent to you. But one dreamt about them at night and I remember having a splendid kind of daydream in which I nursed my beloved Monsieur Adolphe when he had cholera and I gave him, I think, blood transfusions to save his life. How very silly one is. And think of all the other things you think of doing! There was one time when I was quite determined to be a nun and later on I thought I'd be a hospital nurse. Well, I suppose we shall have Mrs Burton-Cox in a moment. I wonder how she will react to you?'

Poirot gazed at his watch.

'We shall be able to see that fairly soon.'

'Have we anything else we ought to talk about first?'

'I think there are a few things we might compare notes on. As I say, there are one or two things that I think could do with investigation. An elephant investigation for you, shall we say? And an understudy for an elephant for me.'

'What an extraordinary thing to say,' said Mrs Oliver. 'I told you I was done with elephants.'

'Ah,' said Poirot, 'but elephants perhaps have not done with you.'

The front doorbell sounded once again. Poirot and Mrs Oliver looked at each other.

'Well,' said Mrs Oliver, 'here we go.'

She left the room once more. Poirot heard sounds of

greeting going on outside and in a moment or two Mrs Oliver returned, ushering the somewhat massive figure of Mrs Burton-Cox.

'What a delightful flat you have,' said Mrs Burton-Cox. 'So charming of you to have spared time – your very valuable time, I'm sure – you asked me to come and see you.' Her eyes shot sideways to Hercule Poirot. A faint expression of surprise passed over her face. For a moment her eyes went from him to the baby grand piano that stood in one window. It occurred to Mrs Oliver that Mrs Burton-Cox was thinking that Hercule Poirot was a piano-tuner. She hastened to dispel this illusion.

'I want to introduce you,' she said, 'to M. Hercule Poirot.' Poirot came forward and bent over her hand.

'I think he is the only person who might be able to help you in some way. You know. What you were asking me about the other day concerning my godchild, Celia Ravenscroft.'

'Oh yes, how kind of you to remember. I do so hope you can give me a little more knowledge of what really happened.'

'I'm afraid I haven't been very successful,' said Mrs Oliver, 'and that is really why I asked M. Poirot to meet you. He is a wonderful person, you know, for information on things generally. Really on top of his profession. I cannot tell you how many friends of mine he has assisted and how many, well, I can really call them mysteries, he has elucidated. And this was such a tragic thing to have happened.'

'Yes, indeed,' said Mrs Burton-Cox. Her eyes were still somewhat doubtful. Mrs Oliver indicated chairs and remarked,

'Now what will you have? A glass of sherry? It's too late for tea, of course. Or would you prefer a cocktail of some kind?'

'Oh, a glass of sherry. You are very kind.'

'Monsieur Poirot?'

'I, too,' said Poirot.

Mrs Oliver could not help being thankful that he had not asked for *Sirop de Cassis* or one of his favourite fruit drinks. She got out glasses and a decanter.

'I have already indicated to Monsieur Poirot the outlines of the enquiry you want to make.'

'Oh yes,' said Mrs Burton-Cox.

She seemed rather doubtful and not so sure of herself

as it would seem she was in the natural habit of being.

'These young people,' she said to Poirot, 'so difficult nowadays. These young people. My son, such a dear boy, we have great hopes of his doing well in the future. And then there is this girl, a very charming girl, who, as probably Mrs Oliver told you, is her goddaughter, and – well, of course one never knows. I mean these friendships spring up and very often they don't last. They are what we used to call calf love, you know, years ago, and it is very important to know a little at least about the – antecedents of people. You know, what their families are like. Oh, of course I know Celia's a very well-born girl and all that, but there *was* this tragedy. Mutual suicide, I believe, but nobody has been really able to enlighten me at all on what led to it or what led up to it, shall we say. I have no actual friends who were friends in common with the Ravenscrofts and so it is very difficult for me to have ideas. I know Celia is a charming girl and all that, but one would like to know, to know more.'

'I understand from my friend, Mrs Oliver, that you wanted to know something specifically. You wanted to know, in fact – '

'What you said you wanted to know,' said Mrs Oliver, chipping in with some firmness, 'was whether Celia's father shot her mother and then himself or whether Celia's mother shot her father and then herself.'

'I feel it makes a difference,' said Mrs Burton-Cox. 'Yes, definitely I feel it makes a difference.'

'A very interesting point of view,' said Poirot.

His tone was not very encouraging.

'Oh, the emotional background, shall I say, the emotional events that led up to all this. In a marriage, you must admit, one has to think of the children. The children, I mean, that are to come. I mean heredity. I think now we realize that heredity does more than environment. It leads to certain formation of character and certain very grave risks that one might not want to take.'

'True,' said Poirot. 'The people who undertake the risks are the ones that have to make the decision. Your son and this young lady, it will be their choice.'

'Oh, I know, I know. Not mine. Parents are never allowed to choose, are they, or even to give any advice. But I would like to know something about it, yes, I would like to know very much. If you feel that you could undertake any –

investigation I suppose is the word you would use. But perhaps – perhaps I am being a very foolish mother. You know. Over-anxious about my dear son. Mothers are like that.'

She gave a little whinney of laughter, putting her head slightly on one side.

'Perhaps,' she said, as she tipped up the sherry glass, 'perhaps you will think about it and I also will let you know. Perhaps the exact points and things that I am worried about.'

She looked at her watch.

'Oh dear. Oh dear, I'm late for another appointment. I shall have to go. I am so sorry, dear Mrs Oliver, to have to run away so soon, but you know what it is. I had great difficulties finding a taxi this afternoon. One after another just turned his head aside and drove straight past me. All very, very difficult, isn't it? I think Mrs Oliver has your address, has she not?'

'I will give you my address,' said Poirot. He removed a card from his pocket and handed it to her.

'Oh yes, yes. I see. Monsieur Hercule Poirot. You are French, is that right?'

'I am Belgian,' said Poirot.

'Oh yes, yes. Belgique. Yes, yes. I quite understand. I am so pleased to have met you and I feel so hopeful. Oh dear, I must go very, very fast.'

Shaking Mrs Oliver warmly by the hand, then extending the same hand to Poirot, she left the room and the door sounded in the hall.

'Well, what do you think of that?' said Mrs Oliver.

'What do you?' said Poirot.

'She ran away,' said Mrs Oliver. 'She ran away. You frightened her in some way.'

'Yes,' said Poirot, 'I think you've judged quite right.'

'She wanted me to get things out of Celia, she wanted me to get some knowledge out of Celia, some expression, some sort of secret she suspected was there, but she doesn't want a real proper investigation, does she?'

'I think not,' said Poirot. 'That is interesting. Very interesting. She is well-to-do, you think?'

'I should say so. Her clothes are expensive, she lives at an expensive address, she is – it's difficult to make out. She's a pushing woman and a bossy woman. She sits on a lot of committees. There's nothing, I mean, suspicious about her. I've asked a few people. Nobody likes her very much. But she's a sort of public-spirited woman who takes part in politics, all those sort of things.'

'Then what is wrong with her?' said Poirot.

'You think there is something wrong with her? Or do you just not like her, like I do?'

'I think there is something there that she does not want to come to light,' said Poirot.

'Oh. And are you going to find out what it is?'

'Naturally, if I can,' said Poirot. 'It may not be easy. She is in retreat. She was in retreat when she left us here. She was afraid of what questions I was going to ask her. Yes. It is interesting.' He sighed. 'One will have to go back, you know, even farther than one thought.'

'What, back into the past again?'

'Yes. Somewhere in the past, in more cases than one, there is something that one will have to know before we can come back again to what happened – what is it now? – fifteen years ago, twenty years ago, at a house called Over-cliffe. Yes. One will have to go back again.'

'Well, that's that,' said Mrs Oliver. 'And now, what is there to do. What is this list of yours?'

'I have heard a certain amount of information through police records on what was found in the house. You will remember that among the things there were four wigs.'

'Yes,' said Mrs Oliver, 'you said that four wigs were too many.'

'It seemed to be a little excessive,' said Poirot. 'I have also got certain useful addresses. The address of a doctor that might be helpful.'

'The doctor? You mean, the family doctor?'

'No, not the family doctor. The doctor who gave evidence at an inquest on a child who met with an accident. Either pushed by an older child or possibly by someone else.'

'You mean by the mother?'

'Possibly the mother, possibly by someone else who was in the house at the time. I know the part of England where that happened, and Superintendent Garroway has been able to trace him, through sources known to him and also through journalistic friends of mine, who were interested in this particular case.'

'And you're going to see – he must be a very old man by now.'

'It is not him I shall go to see, it is his son. His son is

also qualified as a specialist in various forms of mental disorders. I have an introduction to him and he might be able to tell me something interesting. There have also been enquiries into a case of money.'

'What do you mean by money?'

'Well, there are certain things we have to find out. That is one of the things in anything which might be a crime. Money. Who has money to lose by some happening, who has money to gain by something happening. That, one has to find out.'

'Well, they must have found out in the case of the Ravenscrofts.'

'Yes, that was all quite natural, it seems. They had both made normal wills, leaving in each case, the money to the other partner. The wife left her money to the husband and the husband left his money to his wife. Neither of them benefited by what happened because they both died. So that the people who did profit, were the daughter, Celia, and a younger child, Edward, who I gather is now at a university abroad.'

'Well, that won't help. Neither of the children were there or could have had anything to do with it.'

'Oh no, that is quite true. One must go further – further back, further forward, further sideways to find out if there is some financial motive somewhere that is – well, shall we say, significant.'

'Well, don't ask me to do that sort of thing,' said Mrs Oliver, 'I've no real qualifications for that. I mean, that's come up, I suppose, fairly reasonable in the – well, in the elephants that I've talked to.'

'No. I think the best thing for you to do would be to, shall we say, take on the subject of the wigs.'

'Wigs?'

'There had been a note made in the careful police report at the time of the suppliers of the wigs, who were a very expensive firm of hairdressers and wig-makers in London, in Bond Street. Later, that particular shop closed and the business was transferred somewhere else. Two of the original partners continued to run it and I understand it has now been given up, but I have here an address of one of the principal fitters and hairdressers, and I thought perhaps that it would come more easily if enquiries were made by a woman.'

'Ah,' said Mrs Oliver, 'me?'

'Yes, you.'

'All right. What do you want me to do?'

'Pay a visit to Cheltenham to an address I shall give you and there you will find a Madame Rosentelle. A woman no longer young but who was a very fashionable maker of ladies' hair adornments of all kinds, and who was married, I understand, to another in the same profession, a hairdresser who specialized in surmounting the problems of gentlemen's baldness. Toupees and other things.'

'Oh dear,' said Mrs Oliver, 'the jobs you do give me to do. Do you think they'll remember anything about it?'

'Elephants remember,' said Hercule Poirot.

'Oh, and who are you going to ask questions of? This doctor you talked about?'

'For one, yes.'

'And what do you think he'll remember?'

'Not very much,' said Poirot, 'but it seems to me possible that he might have heard about a certain accident. It must have been an interesting case, you know. There must be records of the case history.'

'You mean of the twin sister?'

'Yes. There were two accidents as far as I can hear connected with her. One when she was a young mother living in the country, at Hatters Green I think the address was, and again later when she was in Malaya. Each time an accident which resulted in the death of a child. I might learn something about – '

'You mean that as they were twin sisters, that Molly – my Molly I mean – might also have had mental disability of some kind? I don't believe it for a minute. She wasn't like that. She was affectionate, loving, very good-looking, emotional and – oh, she was a terribly nice person.'

'Yes. Yes, so it would seem. And a happy person on the whole, would you say?'

'Yes. She was a happy person. A *very* happy person. Oh, I know I never saw anything of her later in life, of course; she was living abroad. But it always seemed to me on the very rare occasions when I got a letter or went to see her that she was a happy person.'

'And the twin sister you did not really know?'

'No. Well, I think she was . . . well, quite frankly she was in an institution of some kind, I think, on the rare

117

occasions that I saw Molly. She wasn't at Molly's wedding, not as a bridesmaid even.'

'That is odd in itself.'

'I still don't see what you're going to find out from that.'

'Just information,' said Poirot.

Chapter 14

DR WILLOUGHBY

Hercule Poirot got out of the taxi, paid the fare and a tip, verified the fact that the address he had come to was the address corresponding to that written down in his little notebook, took carefully a letter from his pocket addressed to Dr Willoughby, mounted the steps to the house and pressed the bell. The door was opened by a manservant. On reception of Poirot's name he was told that Dr Willoughby was expecting him.

He was shown into a small, comfortable room with bookshelves up the side of it, there were two armchairs drawn to the fire and a tray with glasses on it and two decanters. Dr Willoughby rose to greet him. He was a man between fifty and sixty with a lean, thin body, a high forehead, dark-haired and with very piercing grey eyes. He shook hands and motioned him to a seat. Poirot produced the letter from his pocket.

'Ah, yes.'

The doctor took it from him, opened it, read it and then, placing it beside him, looked at Poirot with some interest.

'I had already heard,' he said, 'from Superintendent Garroway and also, I may say, from a friend of mine in the Home Office, who also begged me to do what I can for you in the matter that interests you.'

'It is a rather serious favour to ask, I know,' said Poirot, 'but there are reasons which make it important for me.'

'Important for you after this number of years?'

'Yes. Of course I shall quite understand if those particular events have passed out of your mind altogether.'

'I can't say they've done that. I am interested, as you may have heard, in special branches of my profession, and have been for many years.'

'Your father, I know, was a very celebrated authority on them.'

'Yes, he was. It was a great interest in his life. He had a lot of theories, some of them triumphantly proved right and some of them which proved disappointing. It is, I gather, a mental case you are interested in?'

'A woman. Her name was Dorothea Preston-Grey.'

'Yes. I was quite a young man at the time. I was already interested in my father's line of thought although my theories and his did not always agree. The work he did was interesting and the work I did in collaboration interested me very much. I don't know what your particular interest was in Dorothea Preston-Grey, as she was at the time, Mrs Jarrow later.'

'She was one of twins, I gather,' said Poirot.

'Yes. That was at that moment, I may say, my father's particular field of study. There was a project on hand at that time, to follow up the general lives of selected pairs of identical twins. Those who were brought up in the same environment, those who through various chances of life were brought up in entirely different environments. To see how alike they remained, how similar the things were that happened to them. Two sisters, perhaps, or two brothers who had hardly spent any of their life together and yet in an extraordinary way the same things seemed to happen to them at the same time. It was all – indeed it has been all – extremely interesting. However, that is not your interest in the matter, I gather.'

'No,' said Poirot, 'it is a case, I think – the part of it that is to say that I'm interested in – of an accident to a child.'

'That is so. It was in Surrey, I think. Yes, a very pleasant area, that, in which people lived. Not very far from Camberley, I think. Mrs Jarrow was a young widow at that time and she had two small children. Her husband had recently died in an accident. She was, as a result –'

'Mentally disturbed?' asked Poirot.

'No, she was not thought to be so. She was deeply shocked by her husband's death and had a great sense of loss, but she was not recovering very satisfactorily in the impression of her own doctor. He did not quite like the way her convalescence was tending, and she did not seem to be getting over her bereavement in the way that he would have liked. It seemed to be causing her rather peculiar reactions. Anyway, he wanted a consultation and my father was asked by him to come and see what he could make of it. He found her condition interesting, and at the same time he thought it held very decided dangers, and he seemed to think that it would be as well if she was put under observation in some nursing home where particular care could be taken. Things like that. Even more so after the case when this accident to the child happened. There were two children, and according to Mrs Jarrow's account of what happened, it was the older child, a girl, who attacked the little boy who was four or five years younger than she was, hitting him with a garden spade or hoe, so that he fell into an ornamental pond they had in the garden and was drowned. Well, these things, as you know, happen quite often among children. Children are pushed in a perambulator into a pond sometimes because an older child, being jealous, thinks that "Mummy will have so much less trouble if only Edward or Donald, or whatever his name is, wasn't here," or, "It would be much nicer for her." It all results from jealousy. There did not seem to be any particular cause or evidence of jealousy in this case, though. The child had not resented the birth of her brother. On the other hand, Mrs Jarrow had not wanted this second child. Although her husband had been pleased to have this second child coming, Mrs Jarrow did not want it. She had tried two doctors with the idea of having an abortion but did not succeed in finding one who would perform what was then an illegal operation. It was said by one of the servants, and also by a boy who was bringing a telegram, I believe, to the house, that it was a woman who attacked the boy, not the other child. And one of the servants said very definitely she had been looking out of the window and that it was her mistress. She said, "I don't think the poor thing knows what she is doing nowadays. You know, just since the master died she's been in, oh, such a state as never was." Well, as I say, I don't know exactly what you want to know about the case. A verdict was brought in of accident, it was considered to be an accident, and the children had been said to be playing together, pushing each other, etcetera, and that therefore it was undoubtedly a very unfortunate accident. It was left at that, but my father when consulted, and after a conversation with Mrs Jarrow and certain tests, questionnaires, sympathetic remarks to her and questions, he was quite sure she had been responsible for what happened. According to his advice it would be advisable for her to have mental treatment.'

'But your father *was* quite sure that *she* had been responsible?'

'Yes. There was a school of treatment at the time which was very popular and which my father believed in. That school's belief was that after sufficient treatment, lasting sometimes quite a long time, a year or longer, people could resume a normal everyday life, and it was to their advantage to do so. They could be returned to live at home and with a suitable amount of attention, both medical and from those, usually near relatives, who were with them and could observe them living a normal life, everything would go well. This, I may say, did meet with success at first in many cases, but later there was a difference. Several cases had most unfortunate results. Patients who appeared to be cured came home to their natural surroundings, to a family, a husband, their mothers and fathers, and slowly relapsed, so that very often tragedies or near tragedies occurred. One case my father was bitterly disappointed in – also a very important case in his knowledge – was a woman who came back to live with the same friend she lived with before. All seemed to be going happily but after about five or six months she sent urgently for a doctor and when he came said, "I must take you upstairs because you will be angry at what I have done, and you will have to send for the police, I am afraid. I know that must happen. But you see, I was commanded to do this. I saw the Devil looking out of Hilda's eyes. I saw the Devil there so I knew what I had to do. I knew I had to kill her." The woman was lying dead in a chair, strangled, and after her death her eyes had been attacked. The killer died in a mental home with never any feeling about her crime except that it had been a necessary command laid upon her because it was her duty to destroy the Devil.'

Poirot shook his head sadly –

The doctor went on: 'Yes. Well, I consider that in a mild way Dorothea Preston-Grey suffered from a form of mental disorder that was dangerous and that she could only be considered safe if she lived under supervision. This was not generally accepted, I may say, at the time, and my father did consider it most inadvisable. Once she had been committed to a very pleasant nursing home a very good treatment was given. And again, after a period of years she appeared to be completely sane, left the establishment, lived an ordinary life with a very pleasant nurse more or less in charge of her, though considered in the household as a lady's maid. She went about, made friends and sooner or later went abroad.'

'To Malaya,' said Poirot.

'Yes. I see you've been correctly informed. She went to Malaya to stay with her twin sister.'

'And there another tragedy happened?'

'Yes. A child of a neighbour was attacked. It was thought at first by an amah, and afterwards I believe one of the native servants, a bearer, was suspected. But there again there seemed no doubt that Mrs Jarrow had, for one of those mental reasons known only to her, been guilty of the attack. There was no definite evidence, I understand, which could be brought against her. I think General – I forget his name now – '

'Ravenscroft?' said Poirot.

'Yes, yes, General Ravenscroft agreed to arrange for her to go back to England and again undergo medical treatment. Is that what you wanted to know?'

'Yes,' said Poirot, 'that is what I have partly heard already, but mainly I may say, by hearsay, which is not dependable. What I want to ask you was, this was a case concerned with identical twins. What about the other twin? Margaret Preston-Grey. Afterwards the wife of General Ravenscroft. Was she likely to be affected by the same malady?'

'There was never any medical case about her. She was perfectly sane. My father was interested, visited her once or twice and talked to her because he had so often seen cases of almost identical illnesses or mental disturbances happen between identical twins who had started life very devoted to each other.'

'Only started life, you said?'

'Yes. On certain occasions a state of animosity can arise between identical twins. It follows on a first keen protective love one for the other, but it can degenerate into something which is nearer hatred, if there is some emotional strain that could trigger it off or could arouse it, or any emotional crisis to account for animosity arising between two sisters.

'I think there might have been that here. General Ravenscroft as a young subaltern or captain or whatever he was, fell deeply in love, I think, with Dorothea Preston-Grey, who was a very beautiful girl. Actually the more beautiful

122

of the two – she also fell in love with him. They were not officially engaged, but General Ravenscroft transferred his affections fairly soon to the other sister, Margaret. Or Molly as she was called. He fell in love with her, and asked her to marry him. She returned his affection and they were married as soon as it became feasible in his career. My father had no doubt that the other twin, Dolly, was bitterly jealous of her sister's marriage and that she continued to be in love with Alistair Ravenscroft and to resent his marriage. However, she got over it all, married another man in due course – a thoroughly happy marriage, it seemed, and later she used frequently to go to visit the Ravenscrofts, not only on that one occasion in Malaya, but later when they were in another station abroad and after they returned home. She was by that time apparently cured again, was no longer in any kind of mental dejection and lived with a very reliable nurse companion and staff of servants. I believe, or so my father had always told me, that Lady Ravenscroft, Molly, remained very devoted to her sister. She felt very protective towards her and loved her dearly. She wanted often, I think, to see more of her than she did, but General Ravenscroft was not so keen on her doing so. I think it possible that the slightly unbalanced Dolly – Mrs Jarrow – continued to feel a very strong attachment to General Ravenscroft, which I think may have been embarrassing and difficult for him, though I believe that his wife was quite convinced that her sister had got over any feelings of jealousy or anger.'

'I understand Mrs Jarrow was staying with the Ravenscrofts about three weeks or so before the tragedy of their suicide happened.'

'Yes, that was quite true. Her own tragic death happened then. She was quite frequently a sleep-walker. She went out one night walking in her sleep and had an accident, falling down a portion of the cliff to which a pathway which had been discarded appeared to lead. She was found the next day and I believe died in hospital without recovering consciousness. Her sister Molly was extremely upset and bitterly unhappy about this, but I would like to say, which you probably want to know, I do not think that this can in any way be held responsible for the subsequent suicide of the married couple who were living so happily together. Grief for a sister's or a sister-in-law's death would hardly lead you to commit suicide. Certainly not to a double suicide.'

'Unless, perhaps,' said Hercule Poirot, 'Margaret Ravenscroft had been responsible for her sister's death.'

'Good heavens!' said Dr Willoughby – 'surely you are not suggesting – '

'That it was Margaret who followed her sleep-walking sister, and that it was Margaret's hand that was stretched out to push Dorothea over the cliff edge?'

'I refuse absolutely,' said Dr Willoughby, 'to accept any such idea.'

'With people,' said Hercule Poirot, 'one never knows.'

Chapter 15

EUGENE AND ROSENTELLE, HAIR STYLISTS AND BEAUTICIANS

Mrs Oliver looked at Cheltenham with approval. As it happened, she had never been to Cheltenham before. How nice, said Mrs Oliver to herself, to see some houses that are really like houses, proper houses.

Casting her mind back to youthful days, she remembered that she had known people, or at least her relations, her aunts, had known people who lived at Cheltenham. Retired people usually. Army or Navy. It was the sort of place, she thought, where one would like to come and live if one had spent a good deal of time abroad. It had a feeling of English security, good taste and pleasant chat and conversation.

After looking in one or two agreeable antique shops, she found her way to where she wanted – or rather Hercule Poirot wanted her – to go. It was called The Rose Green Hairdressing Saloons. She walked inside it and looked round. Four or five people were in process of having things done to their hair. A plump young lady left her client and came forward with an enquiring air.

'Mrs Rosentelle?' said Mrs Oliver, glancing down at a card. 'I understand she said she could see me if I came here this morning. I don't mean,' she added, 'having anything done to my hair, but I wanted to consult her about something and I believe a telephone call was made and she said if I came at half past eleven she could spare me a short time.'

'Oh yes,' said the girl. 'I think Madam is expecting someone.'

She led the way through a passage down a short flight of steps and pushed a swing door at the bottom of it. From the hairdressing saloon they had passed into what was obviously Mrs Rosentelle's house. The plump girl knocked at the door and said, 'The lady to see you,' as she put her nose in, and then asked rather nervously, 'What name did you say?'

'Mrs Oliver,' said Mrs Oliver.

She walked in. It had a faint effect of what might have been yet another showroom. There were curtains of rose gauze and roses on the wallpaper and Mrs Rosentelle, a woman Mrs Oliver thought of as roughly her own age or possibly a good many years older, was just finishing what was obviously a cup of morning coffee.

'Mrs Rosentelle?' said Mrs Oliver.

'Yes?'

'You did expect me?'

'Oh yes. I didn't quite understand what it was all about. The lines are so bad on the telephone. That is quite all right, I have about half an hour to spare. Would you like some coffee?'

'No, thank you,' said Mrs Oliver. 'I won't keep you any longer than I need. It is just something that I want to ask you about, that you may happen to remember. You have had quite a long career, I understand, in the hairdressing business.'

'Oh yes. I'm quite thankful to give over to the girls now. I don't do anything myself these days.'

'Perhaps you still advise people?'

'Yes, I do that.' Mrs Rosentelle smiled.

She had a nice, intelligent face with well arranged, brown hair, with somewhat interesting grey streaks in it here and there.

'I'm not sure what it's all about.'

'Well, really I wanted to ask you a question about, well, I suppose in a way about wigs generally.'

'We don't do as much in wigs now as we used to do.'

'You had a business in London, didn't you?'

'Yes. First in Bond Street and then we moved to Sloane Street but it's very nice to live in the country after all that, you know. Oh yes, my husband and I are very satisfied here. We run a small business but we don't do much in the wig line nowadays,' she said, 'though my husband does advise and get wigs designed for men who are bald. It really makes a big difference, you know, to many people in their business if they don't look too old and it often helps in getting a job.'

'I can quite imagine that,' said Mrs Oliver.

From sheer nervousness she said a few more things in the way of ordinary chat and wondered how she would start on her subject. She was startled when Mrs Rosentelle leant forward and said suddenly, 'You are Ariadne Oliver, aren't you? The novel writer?'

'Yes,' said Mrs Oliver, 'as a matter of fact – ' she had her usual somewhat shame-faced expression when she said this, that was habitual to her – 'yes, I do write novels.'

'I'm so fond of your books. I've read a lot of them. Oh, this is very nice indeed. Now tell me in what way can I help you?'

'Well, I wanted to talk about wigs and about something that happened a great many years ago and probably you mayn't remember anything about it.'

'Well, I rather wonder – do you mean fashions of years ago?'

'Not exactly. It's a woman, a friend of mine – actually I was at school with her – and then she married and went out to Malaya and came back to England, and there was a tragedy later and one of the things I think that people found surprising after it was that she had so many wigs. I think they had been all supplied by you, by your firm, I mean.'

'Oh, a tragedy. What was her name?'

'Well, her name when I knew her was Preston-Grey, but afterwards her name was Ravenscroft.'

'Oh. Oh yes, that one. Yes, I do remember Lady Ravenscroft. I remember her quite well. She was so nice and really very, very good-looking still. Yes, her husband was a Colonel or a General or something and they'd retired and they lived in – I forget the county now – '

' – And there was what was supposed to be a double suicide,' said Mrs Oliver.

'Yes. Yes, I remember reading about it and saying, "Why that's our Lady Ravenscroft," and then there was a picture of them both in the paper, and I saw that it was so. Of course, I'd never seen him but it was her all right. It seemed so sad, so much grief. I heard that they discovered that she had cancer and they couldn't do anything about it so this happened. But I never heard any details or anything.'

'No,' said Mrs Oliver.

'But what is it you think I can tell you?'

'You supplied her with wigs and I understand the people investigating, I suppose the police, thought four wigs was quite a lot to have, but perhaps people did have four wigs at a time?'

'Well, I think that most people had two wigs at least,' said Mrs Rosentelle. 'You know, one to send back to be serviced, as you might say, and the other one that they wore while it was away.'

'Do you remember Lady Ravenscroft ordering an extra two wigs?'

'She didn't come herself. I think she'd been or was ill in hospital, or something, and it was a French young lady who came. I think a French lady who was companion to her or something like that. Very nice. Spoke perfect English. And she explained all about the extra wigs she wanted, sizes and colours and styles and ordered them. Yes. Fancy my remembering it. I suppose I wouldn't have except that about – oh it must have been a month later – a month, perhaps more, six weeks – I read about the suicide, you know. I'm afraid they gave her bad news at the hospital or wherever she was, and so she just couldn't face living any more, and her husband felt he couldn't face life without her – '

Mrs Oliver shook her head sadly – and continued her enquiries.

'They were different kinds of wigs, I suppose.'

'Yes, one had a very pretty grey streak in it, and then there was a party one and one for evening wear, and one close-cropped with curls. Very nice, that you could wear under a hat and it didn't get messed up. I was sorry not to have seen Lady Ravenscroft again. Even apart from her illness, she had been very unhappy about a sister who had recently died. A twin sister.'

'Yes, twins are very devoted, aren't they,' said Mrs Oliver.

'She'd always seemed such a happy woman before,' said Mrs Rosentelle.

Both women sighed. Mrs Oliver changed the subject.

'Do you think that I'd find a wig useful?' she asked.

The expert stretched out a hand and laid it speculatively on Mrs Oliver's head.

'I wouldn't advise it – you've got a splendid crop of hair – very thick still – I imagine – ' a faint smile came to her lips – 'you enjoy doing things with it?'

'How clever of you to know that. It's quite true – I enjoy experimenting – it's such fun.'

'You enjoy life altogether, don't you?'

'Yes, I do. I suppose it's the feeling that one never knows what might be going to happen next.'

'Yet that feeling,' said Mrs Rosentelle, 'is just what makes so many people never stop worrying!'

Chapter 16

MR GOBY REPORTS

Mr Goby came into the room and sat, as indicated by Poirot, in his usual chair. He glanced around him before choosing what particular piece of furniture or part of the room he was about to address. He settled, as often before, for the electric fire, not turned on at this time of year. Mr Goby had never been known to address the human being he was working for directly. He selected always the cornice, a radiator, a television set, a clock, sometimes a carpet or a mat. Out of a briefcase he took a few papers.

'Well,' said Hercule Poirot, 'you have something for me?'

'I have collected various details,' said Mr Goby.

Mr Goby was celebrated all over London, indeed possibly all over England and even further, as great purveyor of information. How he performed these miracles nobody ever really quite knew. He employed a not excessive staff. Sometimes he complained that his legs, as he sometimes called them, were not as good as they used to be. But his results were still able to astonish people who had commissioned them.

'Mrs Burton-Cox,' he said, announcing the name much as though he had been the local churchwarden having his turn at reading the lessons. He might equally have been saying 'Third verse, fourth chapter, the book of Isaiah.'

'Mrs Burton-Cox,' he said again. 'Married Mr Cecil Aldbury, manufacturer of buttons on a large scale. Rich man. Entered politics, was MP for Little Stansmere. Mr Cecil

Aldbury was killed in a car accident four years after their marriage. The only child of the marriage died in an accident shortly afterwards. Mr Aldbury's estate was inherited by his wife, but was not as much as had been expected since the firm had not been doing well of late years. Mr Aldbury also left quite a considerable sum of money to a Miss Kathleen Fenn, with whom it seemed he had been having intimate relations quite unknown to his wife. Mrs Burton-Cox continued her political career. Some three years after that she adopted a child which had been born to Miss Kathleen Fenn. Miss Kathleen Fenn insisted that the child was the son of the late Mr Aldbury. This, from what I have been able to learn in my enquiries, is somewhat difficult to accept,' continued Mr Goby. 'Miss Fenn had had many relationships, usually with gentlemen of ample means and generous dispositions, but after all, so many people have their price, have they not? I'm afraid this is quite a serious bill I may have to send you in.'

'Continue,' said Hercule Poirot.

'Mrs Aldbury, as she then was, agreed to adopt the child. A short while later she married Major Burton-Cox. Miss Kathleen Fenn became, I may say, a most successful actress and pop singer and made a very large amount of money. She then wrote to Mrs Burton-Cox saying she would be willing to take back the adopted child. Mrs Burton-Cox refused. Mrs Burton-Cox has been living quite comfortably since, I understand, Major Burton-Cox was killed in Malaya. He left her moderately well off. A further piece of information I have obtained is that Miss Kathleen Fenn, who died a very short while ago – eighteen months, I think – left a Will by which her entire fortune, which amounted by then to a considerable sum of money, was left to her natural son Desmond, at present known under the name of Desmond Burton-Cox.'

'Very generous,' said Poirot. 'Of what did Miss Fenn die?'

'My informant tells me that she contracted leukaemia.'

'And the boy has inherited his mother's money?'

'It was left in trust for him to acquire at the age of twenty-five.'

'So he will be independent, will have a substantial fortune? And Mrs Burton-Cox?'

'Has not been happy in her investments, it is understood. She has sufficient to live on but not much more.'

'Has the boy Desmond made a Will?' asked Poirot.

'That,' said Mr Goby, 'I fear I do not know as yet. But I have certain means of finding out. If I do, I will acquaint you with the fact without loss of time.'

Mr Goby took his leave, absent-mindedly bowing a farewell to the electric fire.

About an hour and a half later the telephone rang.

Hercule Poirot, with a sheet of paper in front of him, was making notes. Now and then he frowned, twirled his moustaches, crossed something out and re-wrote it and then proceeded onward. When the telephone rang he picked up the receiver and listened.

'Thank you,' he said, 'that was quick work. Yes . . . yes, I'm grateful. I really do not know sometimes how you manage these things . . . Yes, that sets out the position clearly. It makes sense of something that did not make sense before . . . Yes . . . I gather . . . yes, I'm listening . . . you are pretty sure that that *is* the case. He knows he is adopted . . . but he never has been told who his real mother was . . . yes. Yes, I see . . . Very well. You will clear up the other point too? Thank you.'

He replaced the receiver and started once more writing down words. In half an hour the telephone rang once more. Once again he picked up the phone.

'I'm back from Cheltenham,' said a voice which Poirot had no difficulty in recognizing.

'Ah, *chère madame,* you have returned? You have seen Mrs Rosentelle?'

'Yes. She is nice. Very nice. And you were quite right, you know, she *is* another elephant.'

'Meaning, *chère madame*?'

'I mean that she remembered Molly Ravenscroft.'

'And she remembered her wigs?'

'Yes.'

Briefly she outlined what the retired hairdresser had told her about the wigs.

'Yes,' said Poirot, 'that agrees. That is exactly what Superintendent Garroway mentioned to me. The four wigs that the police found. Curls, an evening type of head-dress, and two other plainer ones. Four.'

'So I really only told you what you knew already?'

'No, you told me something more than that. She said – that is what you told me just now, is it not? – that Lady Ravenscroft wanted two extra wigs to add to the two that she already had and that this was about three weeks to six weeks before the suicide tragedy occurred. Yes, that is interesting, is it not?'

'It's very natural,' said Mrs Oliver. 'I mean, you know that people, women, I mean, may do awful damage to things. To false hair and things of that kind. If it can't be re-dressed and cleaned, if it's got burnt or got stuff spilt on it you can't get out, or it's been dyed and dyed all wrong – something like that – well then, of course you have to get two new wigs or switches or whatever they are. I don't see what makes you excited about that.'

'Not exactly excited,' said Poirot, 'no. It is a point, but the more interesting point is what you have just added. It was a French lady, was it not, who brought the wigs to be copied or matched?'

'Yes. I gathered some kind of companion or something. Lady Ravenscroft had been or was in hospital or in a nursing home somewhere and she was not in good health and she could not come herself to make a choice or anything of that kind.'

'I see.'

'And so her French companion came.'

'Do you know the name of that companion by any chance?'

'No. I don't think Mrs Rosentelle mentioned it. In fact I don't think she knew. The appointment was made by Lady Ravenscroft and the French girl or woman just brought the wigs along for size and matching and all the rest of it, I suppose.'

'Well,' said Poirot, 'that helps me towards the further step that I am about to take.'

'What have *you* learnt?' said Mrs Oliver. 'Have you done *anything*?'

'You are always so sceptical,' said Poirot. 'You always consider that I do nothing, that I sit in a chair and repose myself.'

'Well I think you sit in a chair and think,' admitted Mrs Oliver, 'but I quite agree that you don't often go out and do things.'

'In the near future I think I may possibly go out and do things,' said Hercule Poirot, 'and that will please you. I may even cross the Channel though certainly not in a boat. A plane, I think is indicated.'

'Oh,' said Mrs Oliver. 'Do you want me to come too?'

'No,' said Poirot, 'I think it would be better if I went

alone on this occasion.'

'You really *will* go?'

'Oh yes, oh yes. I will run about with all activity and so you should be pleased with me, madame.'

When he had rung off, he dialled another number which he looked up from a note he had made in his pocket-book. Presently he was connected to the person whom he wished to speak to.

'My dear Superintendent Garroway, it is Hercule Poirot who addresses you. I do not derange you too much? You are not very busy at this moment?'

'No, I am not busy,' said Superintendent Garroway. 'I am pruning my roses, that's all.'

'There is something that I want to ask you. Quite a small thing.'

'About our problem of the double suicide?'

'Yes, about our problem. You said there was a dog in the house. You said that the dog went for walks with the family, or so you understood.'

'Yes, there was some mention made of a dog. I think it may have been either the housekeeper or someone who said that they went for a walk with the dog as usual that day.'

'In examination of the body was there any sign that Lady Ravenscroft had been bitten by a dog? Not necessarily very recently or on that particular day?'

'Well, it's odd you should say that. I can't say I'd have remembered about it if you hadn't mentioned such a thing. But yes, there were a couple of scars. Not bad ones. But again the housekeeper mentioned that the dog had attacked its mistress more than once and bitten her, though not very severely. Look here, Poirot, there was no rabies about, if that's what you are thinking. There couldn't have been anything of that kind. After all she was shot – they were both shot. There was no question of any septic poisoning or danger of tetanus.'

'I do not blame the dog,' said Poirot, 'it was only something I wanted to know.'

'One dog bite was fairly recent, about a week before, I think, or two weeks somebody said. There was no case of necessary injections or anything of that kind. It had healed quite well. What's that quotation?' went on Superintendent Garroway. ' "*The dog it was that died.*" I can't remember where it comes from but — '

'Anyway, it wasn't the dog that died,' said Poirot. 'That wasn't the point of my question. I would like to have known that dog. He was perhaps a very intelligent dog.'

After he had replaced the receiver with thanks to the Superintendent, Poirot murmured: 'An intelligent dog. More intelligent perhaps than the police were.'

Chapter 17

POIROT ANNOUNCES DEPARTURE

Miss Livingstone showed in a guest. 'Mr Hercules Porrett.'

As soon as Miss Livingstone had left the room, Poirot shut the door after her and sat down by his friend, Mrs Ariadne Oliver.

He said, lowering his voice slightly, 'I depart.'

'You do what?' said Mrs Oliver, who was always slightly startled by Poirot's methods of passing on information.

'I depart. I make the departure. I take a plane to Geneva.'

'You sound as though you were UNO or UNESCO or something.'

'No. It is just a private visit that I make.'

'Have you got an elephant in Geneva?'

'Well, I suppose you might look at it that way. Perhaps two of them.'

'I haven't found out anything more,' said Mrs Oliver. 'In fact I don't know who I can go to, to find out any more.'

'I believe you mentioned, or somebody did, that your goddaughter, Celia Ravenscroft, had a young brother.

'Yes. He's called Edward, I think. I've hardly ever seen him. I took him out once or twice from school, I remember. But that was years ago.'

'Where is he now?'

'He's at university, in Canada I think. Or he's taking some engineering course there. Do you want to go and ask him things?'

'No, not at the moment. I should just like to know where he is now. But I gather he was not in the house when this suicide happened?'

'You're not thinking – you're not thinking for a moment that *he* did it, are you? I mean, shot his father and his mother, both of them. I know boys do sometimes. Very queer they are sometimes when they're at a funny age.'

'He was not in the house,' said Poirot. 'That I know already from my police reports.'

'Have you found out anything else interesting? You look quite excited.'

'I am excited in a way. I have found out certain things that may throw light upon what we already know.'

'Well, what throws light on what?'

'It seems to me possible now that I can understand why Mrs Burton-Cox approached you as she did and tried to get you to obtain information for her about the facts of the suicide of the Ravenscrofts.'

'You mean she wasn't just being a nosey-parker?'

'No. I think there was some motive behind it. This is where, perhaps, money comes in.'

'Money? What's money got to do with that? She's quite well off, isn't she?'

'She has enough to live upon, yes. But it seems that her adopted son whom she regards apparently as her true son – he knows that he was adopted although he knows nothing about the family from which he really came. It seems that when he came of age he made a Will, possibly urged by his adopted mother to do so. Perhaps it was merely hinted to him by some friends of hers or possibly by some lawyer that she had consulted. Anyway, on coming of age he may have felt that he might as well leave everything to her, to his adopted mother. Presumably at that time he had nobody else to leave it to.'

'I don't see how that leads to wanting news about a suicide.'

'Don't you? She wanted to discourage the marriage. If young Desmond had a girl-friend, if he proposed to marry her in the near future, which is what a lot of young people do nowadays – they won't wait or think it over. In that case, Mrs Burton-Cox would not inherit the money he left, since the marriage would invalidate any earlier Will, and presumably if he did marry his girl he would make a new Will leaving everything to her and not to his adopted mother.'

'And you mean Mrs Burton-Cox didn't want that?'

'She wanted to find something that would discourage him

from marrying the girl. I think she hoped, and probably really believed as far as that goes, that Celia's mother killed her husband, afterwards shooting herself. That is the sort of thing that might discourage a boy. Even if her father killed her mother, it is still a discouraging thought. It might quite easily prejudice and influence a boy at that age.'

'You mean he'd think that if her father or mother was a murderer, the girl might have murderous tendencies?'

'Not quite as crude as that but that might be the main idea, I should think.'

'But he wasn't rich, was he? An adopted child.'

'He didn't know his real mother's name or who she was, but it seems that his mother, who was an actress and a singer and who managed to make a great deal of money before she became ill and died, wanted at one time to get her child returned to her and when Mrs Burton-Cox would not agree to that, I should imagine she thought about this boy a great deal and decided that she would leave her money to him. He will inherit this money at the age of twenty-five, but it is held in trust for him until then. So of course Mrs Burton-Cox doesn't want him to marry, or only to marry someone that she really approves of or over whom she might have influence.'

'Yes, that seems to me fairly reasonable. She's not a nice woman though, is she?'

'No,' said Poirot, 'I did not think her a very nice woman.'

'And that's why she didn't want you coming to see her and messing about with things and finding out what she was up to.'

'Possibly,' said Poirot.

'Anything else you have learnt?'

'Yes, I have learnt – that is only a few hours ago really – when Superintendent Garroway happened to ring me up about some other small matters, but I did ask him and he told me that the housekeeper, who was elderly, had very bad eyesight.'

'Does that come into it anywhere?'

'It might,' said Poirot. He looked at his watch. 'I think,' he said, 'it is time that I left.'

'You are on your way to catch your plane at the airport?'

'No. My plane does not leave until tomorrow morning. But there is a place I have to visit today – a place that I wish to see with my own eyes. I have a car waiting outside now to take me there – '

'What is it you want to see?' Mrs Oliver asked with some curiosity.

'Not so much to *see* – to *feel*. Yes – that is the right word – to feel and to recognize what it will be that I feel . . .'

Chapter 18

INTERLUDE

Hercule Poirot passed through the gate of the churchyard. He walked up one of the paths, and presently, against a moss-grown wall he stopped, looking down on a grave. He stood there for some minutes looking first at the grave, then at the view of the Downs and sea beyond. Then his eyes came back again. Flowers had been put recently on the grave. A small bunch of assorted wild flowers, the kind of bunch that might have been left by a child, but Poirot did not think that it was a child who had left them. He read the lettering on the grave.

TO THE MEMORY OF
DOROTHEA JARROW Died Sept 15th 1960
ALSO OF
MARGARET RAVENSCROFT Died Oct 3rd 1960
SISTER OF ABOVE
ALSO OF
ALISTAIR RAVENSCROFT Died Oct 3rd 1960
HER HUSBAND
In their Death they were not divided

– – – –

Forgive us our trespasses
As we forgive those that trespass against us
Lord, have Mercy upon us
Christ, have Mercy upon us
Lord, have Mercy upon us

– – – –

Poirot stood there a moment or two. He nodded his head once or twice. Then he left the churchyard and walked by a footpath that led out on to the cliff and along the cliff. Presently he stood still again looking out to the sea.

He spoke to himself.

'I am sure now that I know what happened and why. I understand the pity of it and the tragedy. One has to go back such a long way. *In my end is my beginning,* or should one put it differently? "In my beginning was my tragic end"? The Swiss girl must have known – but will she tell me? The boy believes she will. For their sakes – the girl and the boy. They cannot accept life unless they know.'

Chapter 19

MADDY AND ZELIE

'Mademoiselle Rouselle?' said Hercule Poirot. He bowed.

Mademoiselle Rouselle extended her hand. About fifty, Poirot thought. A fairly imperious woman. Would have her way. Intelligent, intellectual, satisfied, he thought, with life as she had lived it, enjoying the pleasures and suffering the sorrows life brings.

'I have heard your name,' she said. 'You have friends, you know, both in this country and in France. I do not know exactly what I can do for you. Oh, I know that you explained, in the letter that you sent me. It is an affair of the past, is it not? Things that happened. Not exactly things that happened, but the clue to things that happened many, many years ago. But sit down. Yes. Yes, that chair is quite comfortable, I hope. There are some *petit-fours* and the decanter is on the table.'

She was quietly hospitable without any urgency. She was unworried but amiable.

'You were at one time a governess in a certain family,' said Poirot. 'The Preston-Greys. Perhaps now you hardly remember them.'

'Oh yes, one does not forget, you know, things that happen when you were young. There was a girl, and a boy about four or five years younger in the family I went to. They were nice children. Their father became a General in the Army.'

'There was also another sister.'

'Ah yes, I remember. She was not there when I first came. I think she was delicate. Her health was not good.

She was having treatment somewhere.'

'You remember their mother's Christian name?'

'Margaret, I think was one. The other one I am not sure of by now.'

'Dorothea.'

'Ah yes. A name I have not often come across. But they called each other by shorter names. Molly and Dolly. They were identical twins, you know, remarkably alike. They were both very handsome young women.'

'And they were fond of each other?'

'Yes, they were devoted. But we are, are we not, becoming slightly confused? Preston-Grey is not the name of the children I went to teach. Dorothea Preston-Grey married a Major – ah, I cannot remember the name now. Arrow? No, Jarrow. Margaret's married name was –'

'Ravenscroft,' said Poirot.

'Ah, that. Yes. Curious how one cannot remember names. The Preston-Greys are a generation older. Margaret Preston-Grey had been in a *pensionnat* in this part of the world, and when she wrote after her marriage asking Madame Benoît, who ran that *pensionnat,* if she knew of someone who would come to her as nursery-governess to her children, I was recommended. That is how I came to go there. I spoke only of the other sister because she happened to be staying there during part of my time of service with the children. The children were a girl, I think then of six or seven. She had a name out of Shakespeare. I remember. Rosalind or Celia.'

'Celia,' said Poirot.

'And the boy was only about three or four. His name was Edward. A mischievous but lovable child. I was happy with them.'

'And they were happy, I hear, with you. They enjoyed playing with you and you were very kind in your playing with them.'

'*Moi, j'aime les enfants,*' said Mademoiselle Rouselle.

'They called you "Maddy," I believe.'

She laughed.

'Ah, I like hearing that word. It brings back past memories.'

'Did you know a boy called Desmond? Desmond Burton Cox?'

'Ah yes. He lived I think in a house next door or nearly next door. We had several neighbours and the children very often came to play together. His name was Desmond.

Yes, I remember.'

'You were there long, mademoiselle?'

'No. I was only there for three or four years at most.
Then I was recalled to this country. My mother was very
ill. It was a question of coming back and nursing her,
although I knew it would not be perhaps for very long.
That was true. She died a year and a half or two years
at the most after I returned here. After that I started a
small *pensionnat* out here, taking in rather older girls who
wanted to study languages and other things. I did not
visit England again, although for a year or two I kept up
communication with the country. The two children used
to send me a card at Christmas time.'

'Did General Ravenscroft and his wife strike you as a
happy couple?'

'Very happy. They were fond of their children.'

'They were very well suited to each other?'

'Yes, they seemed to me to have all the necessary qualities
to make their marriage a success.'

'You said Lady Ravenscroft was devoted to her twin
sister. Was the twin sister also devoted to her?'

'Well, I had not very much occasion of judging. Frankly,
I thought that the sister – Dolly, as they called her – was
very definitely a mental case. Once or twice she acted in a
very peculiar manner. She was a jealous woman, I think,
and I understood that she had at one time thought she
was engaged, or was going to be engaged, to General Ravenscroft. As far as I could see he'd fallen in love with her first,
then later, however, his affections turned towards her sister,
which was fortunate, I thought, because Molly Ravenscroft
was a well-balanced and very sweet woman. As for Dolly –
sometimes I thought she adored her sister, sometimes that
she hated her. She was a very jealous woman and she decided
too much affection was being shown to the children. There is
one who could tell you about all this better than I. Mademoiselle Meauhourat. She lives in Lausanne and she went to
the Ravenscrofts about a year and a half to two years after
I had to leave. She was with them for some years. Later I
believe she went back as companion to Lady Ravenscroft
when Celia was abroad at school.'

'I am going to see her. I have her address,' said Poirot.

'She knows a great deal that I do not, and she is a
charming and reliable person. It was a terrible tragedy that
happened later. She knows if anyone does what led to it.

She is very discreet. She has never told me anything. Whether she will tell you I do not know. She may do, she may not.'

Poirot stood for a moment or two looking at Mademoiselle Meauhourat. He had been impressed by Mademoiselle Rouselle, he was impressed also by the woman who stood waiting to receive him. She was not so formidable, she was much younger, at least ten years younger, he thought, and she had a different kind of impressiveness. She was alive, still attractive, eyes that watched you and made their own judgment on you, willing to welcome you, looking with kindliness on those who came her way but without undue softness. Here is someone, thought Hercule Poirot, very remarkable.

'I am Hercule Poirot, mademoiselle.'

'I know. I was expecting you either today or tomorrow.'

'Ah. You received a letter from me?'

'No. It is no doubt still in the post. Our posts are a little uncertain. No. I had a letter from someone else.'

'From Celia Ravenscroft?'

'No. It was a letter writen by someone in close touch with Celia. A boy or a young man, whichever we like to regard him as, called Desmond Burton-Cox. He prepared me for your arrival.'

'Ah. I see. He is intelligent and he wastes no time, I think. He was very urgent that I should come and see you.'

'So I gathered. There's trouble, I understand. Trouble that he wants to resolve, and so does Celia. They think you can help them?'

'Yes, and they think that *you* can help *me*.'

'They are in love with each other and wish to marry.'

'Yes, but there are difficulties being put in their way.'

'Ah, by Desmond's mother, I presume. So he lets me understand.'

'There are circumstances, or have been circumstances, in Celia's life that have prejudiced his mother against his early marriage to this particular girl.'

'Ah. Because of the tragedy, for it was a tragedy.'

'Yes, because of the tragedy. Celia has a godmother who was asked by Desmond's mother to try and find out from Celia the exact circumstances under which that suicide occurred.'

'There's no sense in that,' said Mademoiselle Meauhourat. She motioned with her hand. 'Sit down. Please sit down.

I expect we shall have to talk for some little time. Yes, Celia could not tell her godmother – Mrs Ariadne Oliver, the novelist is it not? Yes, I remember. Celia could not give her the information because she has not got the information herself.'

'She was not there when the tragedy occurred, and no one told her anything about it. Is that right?'

'Yes, that is right. It was thought inadvisable.'

'Ah. And do you approve of that decision or disapprove of it?'

'It is difficult to be sure. Very difficult. I've not been sure of it in the years that have passed since then, and there are quite a lot. Celia, as far as I know, has never been worried. Worried, I mean, as to the why and wherefore. She's accepted it as she would have accepted an aeroplane accident or a car accident. Something that resulted in the death of her parents. She spent many years in a *pensionnnat* abroad.'

'Actually I think the *pensionnat* was run by you, Mademoiselle Meauhourat.'

'That is quite true. I have retired recently. A colleague of mine is now taking it on. But Celia was sent out to me and I was asked to find for her a good place for her to continue her education, as many girls do come to Switzerland for that purpose. I could have recommended several places. At the moment I took her into my own.'

'And Celia asked you nothing, did not demand information?'

'No. It was, you see, before the tragedy happened.'

'Oh. I did not quite understand that.'

'Celia came out here some weeks before the tragic occurrence. I was at that time not here myself. I was still with General and Lady Ravenscroft. I looked after Lady Ravenscroft, acting as a companion to her rather than as a governess to Celia, who was still at that moment in boarding-school. But it was suddenly arranged that Celia should come to Switzerland and finish her education there.'

'Lady Ravenscroft had been in poor health, had she not?'

'Yes. Nothing very serious. Nothing as serious as she had herself feared at one time. But she had suffered a lot of nervous strain and shock and general worry.'

'You remained with her?'

'A sister whom I had living in Lausanne received Celia on her arrival and settled her into the institution which was only for about fifteen or sixteen girls, but there she would start her studies and await my return. I returned some three or four weeks later.'

'But you were at Overcliffe at the time it happened.'

'I was at Overcliffe. General and Lady Ravenscroft went for a walk, as was their habit. They went out and did not return. They were found dead, shot. The weapon was found lying by them. It was one that belonged to General Ravenscroft and had been always kept in a drawer in his study. The finger marks of both of them were found on that weapon. There was no definite indication of who had held it last. Impressions of both people, slightly smeared, were on it. The obvious solution was a double suicide.'

'You found no reason to doubt that?'

'The police found no reason, so I believe.'

'Ah,' said Poirot.

'I beg your pardon?' said Mademoiselle Meauhourat.

'Nothing. Nothing. Just something upon which I reflect.'

Poirot looked at her. Brown hair as yet hardly touched with grey, lips closed firmly together, grey eyes, a face which showed no emotion. She was in control of herself completely.

'So you cannot tell me anything more?'

'I fear not. It was a long time ago.'

'You remember that time well enough.'

'Yes. One cannot entirely forget such a sad thing.'

'And you agreed that Celia should not be told anything more of what had led up to this?'

'Have I not just told you that I had no extra information?'

'You were there, living at Overcliffe, for a period of time before the tragedy, were you not? Four or five weeks — six weeks perhaps.'

'Longer than that, really. Although I had been governess to Celia earlier, I came back this time, after she went to school, in order to help Lady Ravenscroft.'

'Lady Ravenscroft's sister was living with her also about that time, was she not?'

'Yes. She had been in hospital having special treatment for some time. She had shown much improvement and the authorities had felt — the medical authorities I speak of — that she would do better to lead a normal life with her own relations and the atmosphere of a home. As Celia had gone to school, it seemed a good time for Lady Ravenscroft to invite her sister to be with her.'

'Were they fond of each other, those two sisters?'

'It was difficult to know,' said Mademoiselle Meauhourat. Her brows drew together. It was as though what Poirot had just said aroused her interest. 'I have wondered, you know. I have wondered so much since, and at the time really. They were identical twins, you know. They had a bond between them, a bond of mutual dependence and love and in many ways they were very alike. But there were ways also in which they were not alike.'

'You mean? I should be glad to know just what you mean by that.'

'Oh, this has nothing to do with the tragedy. Nothing of that kind. But there was a definite, as I shall put it, a definite physical or mental flaw – whichever way you like to put it – some people nowadays hold the theory that there is some physical cause for any kind of mental disorder. I believe that it is fairly well recognized by the medical profession that identical twins are born either with a great bond between them, a great likeness in their characters which means that although they may be divided in their environment, where they are brought up, the same things will happen to them at the same time of life. They will take the same trend. Some of the cases quoted as medical example seem quite extraordinary. Two sisters, one living in Europe, one say in France, the other in England, they have a dog of the same kind which they choose at about the same date. They marry men singularly alike. They give birth perhaps to a child almost within a month of each other. It is as though they have to follow the pattern wherever they are and without knowing what the other one is doing. Then there is the opposite to that. A kind of revulsion, a hatred almost, that makes one sister draw apart, or one brother reject the other as though they seek to get away from the sameness, the likeness, the knowledge, the things they have in common. And that can lead to very strange results.'

'I know,' said Poirot. 'I have heard of it. I have seen it once or twice. Love can turn to hate very easily. It is easier to hate where you have loved than it is to be indifferent where you have loved.'

'Ah, you know that,' said Mademoiselle Meauhourat.

'Yes, I have seen it not once but several times. Lady Ravenscroft's sister was very like her?'

'I think she was still very like her in appearance, though, if I may say so, the expression on her face was very different. She was in a condition of strain as Lady Ravenscroft was not. She had a great aversion to children. I don't know why. Perhaps she had had a miscarriage in early life. Perhaps she had longed for a child and never had one, but she had a kind of resentment against children. A dislike of them.'

'That had led to one or two rather serious happenings, had it not?' said Poirot.

'Someone has told you that?'

'I have heard things from people who knew both sisters when they were in Malaya. Lady Ravenscroft was there with her husband and her sister, Dolly, came out to stay with them there. There was an accident to a child there, and it was thought that Dolly might have been partially responsible for it. Nothing was proved definitely, but I gather that Molly's husband took his sister-in-law home to England and she had once more to go into a mental home.'

'Yes, I believe that is a very good account of what happened. I do not of course know it of my own knowledge.'

'No, but there are things you do know, I think, from your own knowledge.'

'If so, I see no reason for bringing them back to mind now. Is it not better to leave things when at least they have been accepted?'

'There are other things that could have happened that day at Overcliffe. It may have been a double suicide, it could have been a murder, it could have been several other things. You were told what had happened, but I think from one little sentence you just said, that you know what happened of your own knowledge. You know what happened that day and I think you know what happened perhaps – or began to happen, shall we say? – some time before that. The time when Celia had gone to Switzerland and you were still at Overcliffe. I will ask you one question. I would like to know what your answer would be to it. It is not a thing of direct information, it is a question of what you believe. What were the feelings of General Ravenscroft towards those two sisters, the twin sisters?'

'I know what you mean.'

For the first time her manner changed slightly. She was no longer on her guard, she leaned forward now and spoke to Poirot almost as though she definitely found a relief in doing so.

'They were both beautiful,' she said, 'as girls. I heard that from many people. General Ravenscroft fell in love with Dolly, the mentally afflicted sister. Although she had a disturbed personality she was exceedingly attractive – sexually attractive. He loved her very dearly, and then I don't know whether he discovered in her some characteristic, something perhaps that alarmed him or in which he found a repulsion of some kind. He saw perhaps the beginnings of insanity in her, the dangers connected with her. His affections went to her sister. He fell in love with the sister and married her.'

'He loved them both, you mean. Not at the same time but in each case there was a genuine fact of love.'

'Oh, yes, he was devoted to Molly, relied on her and she on him. He was a very lovable man.'

'Forgive me,' said Poirot, 'you too were in love with him, I think.'

'You – you dare say that to me?'

'Yes. I dare say it to you. I am not suggesting that you and he had a love-affair, nothing of that kind. I'm only saying that you loved him.'

'Yes,' said Zélie Meauhourat. 'I loved him. In a sense, I still love him. There's nothing to be ashamed of. He trusted me and relied on me, but he was never in love with me. You can love and serve and still be happy. I wanted no more than I had. Trust, sympathy, belief in me – '

'And you did,' said Poirot, 'what you could to help him in a terrible crisis in his life. There are things you do not wish to tell me. There are things that I will say to you, things that I have gathered from various information that has come to me, that I know something about. Before I have come to see you I have heard from others, from people who have known not only Lady Ravenscroft, not only Molly, but who have known Dolly. And I know something of Dolly, the tragedy of her life, the sorrow, the unhappiness and also the hatred, the streak perhaps of evil, the love of destruction that can be handed down in families. If she loved the man she was engaged to she must have, when he married her sister, felt hatred perhaps towards that sister. Perhaps she never quite forgave her. But what of Molly Ravenscroft? Did she dislike her sister? Did she hate her?'

'Oh no,' said Zélie Meauhourat, 'she loved her sister.

She loved her with a very deep and protective love. That I do know. It was she who always asked that her sister should come and make her home with her. She wanted to save her sister from unhappiness, from danger too, because her sister would often relapse into fits of rather dangerous rages. She was frightened sometimes. Well, you know enough. You have already said that there was a strange dislike of children from which Dolly suffered.'

'You mean that she disliked Celia?'

'No, no, not Celia. The other one, Edward. The younger one. Twice Edward had dangers of an accident. Once, some kind of tinkering with a car and once some outburst of violent annoyance. I know Molly was glad when Edward went back to school. He was very young, remember, much younger than Celia. He was only eight or nine, at preparatory school. He was vulnerable. Molly was frightened about him.'

'Yes,' said Poirot, 'I can understand that. Now, if I may I will talk of wigs. Wigs. The wearing of wigs. Four wigs. That is a lot for one woman to possess at one time. I know what they were like, what they looked like. I know that when more were needed, a French lady went to the shop in London and spoke about them and ordered them. There was a dog, too. A dog who went for a walk on the day of the tragedy with General Ravenscroft and his wife. Earlier that dog, some little time earlier, had bitten his mistress, Molly Ravenscroft.'

'Dogs are like that,' said Zélie Meauhourat. 'They are never quite to be trusted. Yes, I know that.'

'And I will tell you what I think happened on that day, and what happened before that. Some little time before that.'

'And if I will not listen to you?'

'You will listen to me. You may say that what I have imagined is false. Yes, you might even do that, but I do not think you will. I am telling you, and I believe it with all my heart, that what is needed here is the truth. It is not just imagining, it is not just wondering. There is a girl and a boy who care for each other and who are frightened of the future because of what may have happened and what there might be handed down from the father or the mother to the child. I am thinking of the girl, Celia. A rebellious girl, spirited, difficult perhaps to manage but with brains, a good mind, capable of happiness, capable

146

of courage but needing – there are people who need – truth. Because they can face truth without dismay. They can face it with that brave acceptance you have to have in life if life is to be any good to you. And the boy that she loves, he wants that for her too. Will you listen to me?'

'Yes,' said Zélie Meauhourat, 'I am listening. You understand a great deal, I think, and I think you know more than I could have imagined you would know. Speak and I will listen.'

Chapter 20

COURT OF ENQUIRY

Once more Hercule Poirot stood on the cliff overlooking the rocks below and the sea breaking against them. Here where he stood the bodies of a husband and wife had been found. Here, three weeks before that a woman had walked in her sleep and fallen to her death.

'Why had these things happened?' That had been Superintendent Garroway's question.

Why? What had led to it?

An accident first – and three weeks later a double suicide. Old sins that had left long shadows. A beginning that had led years later to a tragic end.

Today there would be people meeting here. A boy and a girl who sought the Truth. Two people who knew the truth.

Hercule Poirot turned away from the sea and back along the narrow path that led to a house once called Overcliffe.

It was not very far. He saw cars parked against a wall. He saw the outline of a house against the sky. A house that was clearly empty – that needed repainting. A house agent's board hung there – announcing that 'this desirable property' was for sale. On the gate the word Overcliffe had a line drawn over it and the name Down House replaced it. He went to meet two people who were walking towards him. One was Desmond Burton-Cox and the other was Celia Ravenscroft.

'I got an order from the house agent,' said Desmond, 'saying we wanted to view it or however they put it. I've got the key in case we want to go inside. It's changed hands twice in the last five years. But there wouldn't be anything to see there now, would there?'

'I shouldn't think so,' said Celia. 'After all, it's belonged to lots of people already. Some people called Archer who first bought it, and then somebody called Fallowfield, I think. They said it was too lonely. And now these last people are selling it too. Perhaps they were haunted.'

'Do you really believe in haunted houses?' said Desmond.

'Well now, of course I don't think so really,' said Celia, 'but this might be, mightn't it? I mean, the sort of things that happened, the sort of place it is and everything . . .'

'I do not think so,' said Poirot. 'There was sorrow here and Death, but there was also Love.'

A taxi came along the road.

'I expect that's Mrs Oliver,' said Celia. 'She said she'd come by train and take a taxi from the station.'

Two women got out of the taxi. One was Mrs Oliver and with her was a tall, elegantly dressed woman. Since Poirot knew she was coming he was not taken by surprise. He watched Celia to see if she had any reactions.

'Oh!' Celia sprang forward.

She went towards the woman and her face had lit up.

'Zélie!' she said, 'it *is* Zélie? It is really Zélie! Oh, I am so pleased. I didn't know you were coming.'

'Monsieur Hercule Poirot asked me to come.'

'I see,' said Celia. 'Yes, yes, I suppose I see. But I–I didn't–' she stopped. She turned her head and looked at the handsome boy standing beside her. 'Desmond, was it–was it you?'

'Yes. I wrote to Mademoiselle Meauhourat–to Zélie, if I may still call her that.'

'You can always call me that, both of you,' said Zélie. 'I was not sure I wanted to come, I did not know if I was wise to come. That I still do not know, but I hope so.'

'I want to *know*,' said Celia. 'We both want to know. Desmond thought you could tell us something.'

'Monsieur Poirot came to see me,' said Zélie. 'He persuaded me to come today.'

Celia linked her arm in Mrs Oliver's.

'I wanted you to come too because you put this in hand, didn't you? You got Monsieur Poirot and you found out some things yourself, didn't you?'

'People told me things,' said Mrs Oliver, 'people whom

I thought might remember things. Some of them did remember things. Some of them remembered them right and some of them remembered them wrong. That was confusing. Monsieur Poirot says that that does not really matter.'

'No,' said Poirot, 'it is just as important to know what is hearsay and what is certain knowledge. Because from one you can learn facts even if they are not quite the right facts or had not got the explanation that you think they had. With the knowledge that you got from me, madame, from the people whom you designated elephants –' he smiled a little.

'Elephants?!' said Mademoiselle Zélie.

'It is what she called them,' said Poirot.

'Elephants can remember,' explained Mrs Oliver. 'That was the idea I started on. And people can remember things that happened a long time ago just like elephants can. Not all people, of course, but they can usually remember *something*. There were a lot of people who did. I turned a lot of the things I heard over to Monsieur Poirot and he – he has made a sort of – oh, if he was a doctor I should call it a sort of diagnosis, I suppose.'

'I made a list,' said Poirot. 'A list of things that seemed to be pointers to the truth of what happened all those years ago. I shall read the various items to you to see perhaps if you who were concerned in all this, feel that they have any significance. You may not see their significance or you may see it plainly.'

'One wants to know,' said Celia. 'Was it suicide, or was it murder? Did somebody – some outside person – kill both my father and my mother, shoot them for some reason we don't know about, some motive. I shall always think there was something of that kind or something else. It's difficult, but –'

'We will stay here, I think,' said Poirot. 'We will not go into the house as yet. Other people have lived in it and it has a different atmosphere. We will perhaps go in if we wish when we have finished our court of enquiry here.'

'It's a court of enquiry, is it?' said Desmond.

'Yes. A court of enquiry into what happened.'

He moved towards some iron seats which stood near the shelter of a large magnolia near the house. Poirot took from the case he carried a sheet of paper with writing on it. He said to Celia:

'To you, it has got to be that way? A definite choice.

Suicide or murder.'

'One of them must be true,' said Celia.

'I shall say to you that both are true, and more than those two. According to my ideas, we have here not only a murder and also a suicide, but we have as well what I shall call an execution, and we have a tragedy also. A tragedy of two people who loved each other and who died for love. A tragedy of love may not always belong to Romeo and Juliet, it is not necessarily only the young who suffer the pains of love and are ready to die for love. No. There is more to it than that.'

'I don't understand,' said Celia.

'Not yet.'

'Shall I understand?' said Celia.

'I think so,' said Poirot. 'I will tell you what I think happened and I will tell you how I came to think so. The first thing that struck me was the things that were not explained by the evidence that the police examined. Some things were very commonplace, were not evidence at all, you'd think. Among the possessions of the dead Margaret Ravenscroft, were four wigs.' He repeated with emphasis. '*Four* wigs.' He looked at Zélie.

'She did not use a wig all the time,' said Zélie. 'Only occasionally. If she travelled or if she'd been out and got very dishevelled and wanted to tidy herself in a hurry, or sometimes she'd use one that was suitable for evening wear.'

'Yes,' said Poirot, 'it was quite the fashion at that particular date. People certainly when they travelled abroad usually had a wig or two wigs. But in her possession were *four* wigs. Four wigs seemed to me rather a lot. I wondered *why* she needed four. According to the police whom I asked, it was not that she had any tendency to baldness, she had the ordinary hair a woman of her age would have and in good condition. All the same, I wondered about those. One of the wigs had a grey streak in it, I learnt later. It was her hairdresser who told me that. And one of the wigs had little curls. It was the latter wig she was wearing the day she died.'

'Is that significant in any way?' asked Celia. 'She might have been wearing any of them.'

'She might. I also learnt the housekeeper told the police that she had been wearing that particular wig almost all the time for the last few weeks before she died. It appeared to be her favourite one.'

'I can't see –'

'There was also a saying that Superintendent Garroway quoted to me – "Same man, different hat". It gave me furiously to think.'

Celia repeated, 'I don't see –'

Poirot said, 'There was also the evidence of the dog –'

'The dog – what did the dog do?'

'The dog bit her. The dog was said to be devoted to its mistress – but in the last few weeks of her life, the dog turned on her more than once and bit her quite severely.'

'Do you mean it knew she was going to commit suicide?' Desmond stared.

'No, something much simpler than that –'

'I don't –'

Poirot went on – 'No, it knew what no one else seemed to know. It knew she was not its mistress. She looked like its mistress – the housekeeper who was slightly blind and also deaf saw a woman who wore Molly Ravenscroft's clothes and the most recognizable of Molly Ravenscroft's wigs – the one with little curls all over the head. The housekeeper said only that her mistress had been rather different in her manner the last few weeks of her life – "Same man, different hat," had been Garroway's phrase. And the thought – the conviction – came to me then. Same *wig* – different *woman*. The dog knew – he knew by what his nose told him. A different woman, not the woman he loved – a woman whom he disliked and feared. And I thought, suppose that woman was not Molly Ravenscroft – but who could she be? Could she be Dolly – the twin sister?'

'But that's impossible,' said Celia.

'No – it was not impossible. After all, remember, they were twins. I must come now to the things that were brought to my notice by Mrs Oliver. The things people told her or suggested to her. The knowledge that Lady Ravenscroft had recently been in hospital or in a nursing home and that she perhaps had known that she suffered from cancer, or thought that she did. Medical evidence was against that, however. She still might have thought she did, but it was not the case. Then I learnt little by little the early history of her and her twin sister, who loved each other very devotedly as twins do, did everything alike, wore clothes alike, the same things seemed to happen to them, they had illnesses at the same time, they married about the same time or not very far removed in time. And eventually, as many twins do, instead of wanting to do everything in the same fashion and the same way, they wanted to do the opposite. To be as unlike each other as they could. And even between them grew a certain amount of dislike. More than that. There was a reason in the past for that. Alistair Ravenscroft as a young man fell in love with Dorothea Preston-Grey, the elder twin of the two. But his affection shifted to the other sister, Margaret, whom he married. There was jealousy then, no doubt, which led to an estrangement between the sisters. Margaret continued to be deeply attached to her twin, but Dorothea no longer was devoted in any way to Margaret. That seemed to me to be the explanation of a great many things. Dorothea was a tragic figure. By no fault of her own but by some accident of genes, of birth, of hereditary characteristics, she was always mentally unstable. At quite an early age she had, for some reason which has never been made clear, a dislike of children. There is every reason to believe that a child came to its death through her action. The evidence was not definite, but it was definite enough for a doctor to advise that she should have mental treatment, and she was for some years treated in a mental home. When reported cured by doctors, she resumed normal life, came often to stay with her sister and went out to Malaya at a time when they were stationed out there, to join them there. And there, again, an accident happened. A child of a neighbour. And again, although perhaps there was no very definite proof, it seems again Dorothea might have been responsible for it. General Ravenscroft took her home to England and she was placed once more in medical care. Once again she appeared to be cured, and after psychiatric care it was again said that she could go once more and resume a normal life. Margaret believed this time that all would be well, and thought that she ought to live with them so that they could watch closely for any signs of any further mental disability. I don't think that General Ravenscroft approved. I think he had a very strong belief that just as someone can be born deformed, spastic or crippled in some way, she had a deformity of the brain which would recur from time to time and that she would have to be constantly watched and saved from herself in case some other tragedy happened.'

'Are you saying,' asked Desmond, 'that it was *she* who shot both the Ravenscrofts?'

'No,' said Poirot, 'that is not my solution. I think what

happened was that Dorothea killed her sister, Margaret. They walked together on the cliff one day and Dorothea pushed Margaret over. The dormant obsession of hatred and resentment of the sister who, though so like herself, was sane and healthy, was too much for her. Hate, jealousy, the desire to kill all rose to the surface and dominated her. I think that there was one outsider who knew, who was here at the time that this happened. I think *you* knew, Mademoiselle Zélie.'

'Yes,' said Zélie Meauhourat, 'I knew. I was here at the time. The Ravenscrofts had been worried about her. That is when they saw her attempt to injure their small son, Edward. Edward was sent back to school and I and Celia went to my *pensionnat*. I came back here – after seeing Celia settled in. Once the house was empty except for myself, General Ravenscroft and Dorothea and Margaret, nobody had any anxiety. And then one day *it happened*. The two sisters went out together. Dolly returned alone. She seemed in a very queer and nervous state. She came in and sat down at the tea-table. It was then General Ravenscroft noticed that her right hand was covered with blood. He asked her if she had had a fall. She said, "Oh no, it was nothing. Nothing at all. I got scratched by a rose-bush." But there were no rose-bushes on the downs. It was a purely foolish remark and we were worried. If she had said a gorse bush, we might have accepted the remark. General Ravenscroft went out and I went after him. He kept saying as he walked, "Something has happened to Margaret. I'm sure something has happened to Molly." We found her on a ledge a little way down the cliff. She had been battered with a rock and stones. She was not dead but she had bled heavily. For a moment we hardly knew what we could do. We dared not move her. We must get a doctor, we felt, at once, but before we could do that she clung to her husband. She said, gasping for breath, "Yes, it was Dolly. She didn't know what she was doing. She didn't *know*, Alistair. You mustn't let her suffer for it. She's never known the things she does or why. She can't help it. She's never been able to help it. You must promise me, Alistair. I think I'm dying now. No – no, we won't have time to get a doctor and a doctor couldn't do anything. I've been lying here bleeding to death – and I'm very close to death. I know that, but promise me. *Promise* me you'll save her. Promise me you won't let the police arrest her. Promise me that

153

she'll not be tried for killing me, not shut up for life as a criminal. Hide me somewhere so that my body won't be found. Please, please, it's the last thing I ask you. You whom I love more than anything in the world. If I could live for you I would, but I'm not going to live. I can feel that. I crawled a little way but that was all I could do. Promise me. And you, Zélie, you love me too. I know. You've loved me and been good to me and looked after me always. And you loved the children, so you *must* save Dolly. You must save poor Dolly. Please, please. For all the love we have for each other, Dolly must be saved."'

'And then,' said Poirot, 'what did you do? It seems to me that you must in some way between you –'

'Yes. She died, you know. She died within about ten minutes of those last words, and I helped him. I helped him to hide her body. It was a place a little further along the cliff. We carried her there and there were rocks and boulders and stones, and we covered her body as best we could. There was no path to it really, or no way. You had to scramble. We put her there. All Alistair said again and again was – "I promised her. I must keep my word. I don't know how to do it, I don't know how anyone can save her. I don't know. But – " Well, we did do it. Dolly was in the house. She was frightened, desperate with fright – but at the same time she showed a horrible kind of satisfaction. She said, "I always knew, I've known for years that Molly was really evil. She took you away from me, Alistair. You belonged to me – but she took you away from me and made you marry her and I always knew one day I should get even with her. I always knew. Now I'm frightened. What'll they do to me – what'll they say? I can't be shut up again. I can't, I can't. I shall go mad. You won't let me be shut up. They'll take me away and they'll say I'm guilty of murder. It wasn't murder. I just had to do it. Sometimes I do have to do things. I wanted to see the blood, you know. I couldn't wait to see Molly die, though. I ran away. But I knew she would die. I just hoped you wouldn't find her. She just fell over the cliff. People would say it was an accident."'

'It's a horrible story,' said Desmond.

'Yes,' said Celia, 'it's a horrible story, but it's better to know. It's better to know, isn't it? I can't even feel sorry for her. I mean for my mother. I know she was sweet. I know there was never any trace of evil in her – she was good all through – and I know, I can understand, why my father didn't want to marry Dolly. He wanted to marry my mother because he loved her and he had found out by then that there was something wrong with Dolly. Something bad and twisted. But how – how did you do it all?'

'We told a good many lies,' said Zélie. 'We hoped the body would not be found so that later perhaps it might be removed in the night or something like that to somewhere where it could look as though she'd fallen down into the sea. But then we thought of the sleep-walking story. What we had to do was really quite simple. Alistair said, "It's frightening, you know. But I promised – I swore to Molly when she was dying. I swore I'd do as she asked – there's a way, a possible way to save Dolly, if only Dolly can do her part. I don't know if she's capable of it." I said, "Do what?" And Alistair said, "Pretend she's Molly and that it's Dorothea who walked in her sleep and fell to her death."

'We managed it. Took Dolly to an empty cottage we knew of and I stayed with her there for some days. Alistair said Molly had been taken to hospital suffering from shock after the discovery that her sister had fallen over the cliff whilst walking in her sleep at night. Then we brought Dolly back – brought her back as Molly – wearing Molly's clothes and Molly's wig. I got extra wigs – the kind with the curls which really did disguise her. The dear old housekeeper, Janet, couldn't see very well. Dolly and Molly were really very much alike, you know, and their voices were alike. Everyone accepted quite easily that it was Molly, behaving rather peculiarly now and then because of still suffering from shock. It all seemed quite natural. That was the horrible part of it –'

'But how could she keep it up?' asked Celia. 'It must have been dreadfully difficult.'

'No – she did not find it difficult – she had got, you see, what she wanted – what she had always wanted. She had got Alistair –'

'But Alistair – how could he bear it?'

'He told me why and how – on the day he had arranged for me to go back to Switzerland. He told me what I had to do and then he told me what he was going to do.

'He said: "There is only one thing for me to do. I promised Margaret that I wouldn't hand Dolly over to the police, that it should never be known that she was a murderess, that the children were never to know that they had a murderess for an aunt. No one need ever know that Dolly committed murder. She walked in her sleep and fell over the cliff – a sad accident and she will be buried here in the church, and under her own name."

' "How can you let that be done?" I asked – I couldn't bear it.

'He said: "Because of what I am going to do – you have got to know about it."

' "You see," he said, "Dolly has to be stopped from living. If she's near children she'll take more lives – poor soul; she's not fit to live. But you must understand, Zélie, that because of what I am going to do, I must pay with my own life, too – I shall live here quietly for a few weeks with Dolly playing the part of my wife – and then there will be another tragedy – "

'I didn't understand what he meant – I said, "Another accident? Sleep-walking again?" And he said, "No – what will be known to the world is that I and Molly have both committed suicide – I don't suppose the reason will ever be known. They may think it's because she was convinced she had cancer – or that I thought so – all sorts of things may be suggested. But you see – you must help me, Zélie. You are the only person who really loves me and loves Molly and loves the children. If Dolly has got to die, I am the only person who must do it. She won't be unhappy or frightened. I shall shoot her and then myself. Her fingerprints will show on the revolver because she handled it not long ago, and mine will be there too. Justice has to be done and I have to be the executioner. The thing I want you to know is that I did – that I still do – love them both. Molly more than my life. Dolly because I pity her so much for what she was born to be." He said, "Always remember that – " '

Zélie rose and came towards Celia. 'Now you know the truth,' she said. 'I promised your father that you should never know – I have broken my word. I never meant to reveal it to you or to anyone else. Monsieur Poirot made me feel differently. But – it's such a horrible story – '

'I understand how you felt,' said Celia. 'Perhaps you were right from your point of view, but I – I am glad to know because now a great burden seems to have been lifted off me – '

'Because now,' said Desmond, 'we both know. And it's

something we'll never mind about knowing. It *was* a tragedy. As Monsieur Poirot here has said, it was a real tragedy of two people who loved each other. But they didn't kill each other, because they loved each other. One was murdered and the other executed a murderer for the sake of humanity so that more children shouldn't suffer. One can forgive him if he was wrong, but I don't think it *was* wrong really.'

'She was a frightening woman always,' said Celia. 'Even when I was a child I was frightened of her but I didn't know why. But I do know why now. I think my father was a brave man to do what he did. He did what my mother asked him to do, begged him to do with her dying breath. He saved her twin sister whom I think she'd always loved very dearly. I like to think – oh, it seems a silly thing for me to say – ' she looked doubtfully at Hercule Poirot. 'Perhaps you won't think so. I expect you're a Catholic, but it's what's written on their tombstone. "In death they were not divided." It doesn't mean that they died together, but I think they *are* together. I think they came together afterwards. Two people who loved each other very much, and my poor aunt whom I'll try to feel more kindly about than I ever did – my poor aunt didn't have to suffer for what she couldn't perhaps help herself doing. Mind you,' said Celia, suddenly breaking into her ordinary everyday voice, 'she wasn't a nice person. You can't help not liking people if they're not nice people. Perhaps she *could* have been different if she tried, but perhaps she couldn't. And if so, one has to think of her as someone who was very ill – like somebody, for instance, who had plague in a village and they wouldn't let her go out or feed her and she couldn't go amongst other people because the whole village would have died. Something like that. But I'll try and be sorry for her. And my mother and father – I don't worry about them any more. They loved each other so much, and loved poor, unhappy, hating Dolly.'

'I think, Celia,' said Desmond, 'we'd better get married now as soon as possible. I can tell you one thing. My mother is never going to hear anything about this. She's not my own mother and she's not a person I can trust with this sort of secret.'

'Your adopted mother, Desmond,' said Poirot, 'I have good reason to believe was anxious to come between you and Celia and tried to influence you in the idea that from her mother and father she might have inherited some terrible characteristic. But you know, or you may not know and I see no reason why I should not tell you, you will inherit from the woman who was your real mother and who died not very long ago leaving all her money to you – you will inherit a very large sum when you reach the age of twenty-five.'

'If I marry Celia, of course we shall need the money to live on,' said Desmond. 'I quite understand. I know my present adopted mother is very keen on money and I often lend her money even now. She suggested my seeing a lawyer the other day because she said it was very dangerous now that I was over twenty-one, not leaving a Will behind me. I suppose she thought she'd get the money. I had thought of probably leaving nearly all the money to her. But of course now Celia and I are getting married I shall leave it to Celia – and I didn't like the way my mother tried to put me against Celia.'

'I think your suspicions are entirely correct,' said Poirot. 'I dare say she could tell herself that she meant it all for the best, that Celia's origin is something that you ought to know if there is a risk for you to take, but –'

'All right,' said Desmond, 'but – I know I'm being unkind. After all, she adopted me and brought me up and all the rest of it and I dare say if there's enough money I can settle some of it on her. Celia and I will have the rest and we're going to be happy together. After all, there are things that'll make us feel sad from time to time but we shan't worry any more, shall we, Celia?'

'No,' said Celia, 'we'll never worry again. I think they were rather splendid people, my mother and father. Mother tried to look after her sister all her life, but I suppose it was a bit too hopeless. You can't stop people from being like they are.'

'Ah, dear children,' said Zélie. 'Forgive me for calling you children because you are not. You are a grown man and woman. I know that. I am so pleased to have seen you again and to know I have not done any harm in what I did.'

'You haven't done any harm at all and it's lovely seeing you, dear Zélie.' Celia went to her and hugged her. 'I've always been terribly fond of you,' she said.

'And I was very fond of you too when I knew you,' said Desmond. 'When I lived next door. You had lovely games you played with us.'

The two young people turned.

'Thank you, Mrs Oliver,' said Desmond. 'You've been very kind and you've put in a lot of work. I can see that. Thank you, Monsieur Poirot.'

'Yes, thank you,' said Celia. 'I'm very grateful.'

They walked away and the others looked after them.

'Well,' said Zélie, 'I must leave now.' She said to Poirot, 'What about you? Will you have to tell anyone about this?'

'There is one person I might tell in confidence. A retired police force officer. He is no longer actively in the Service now. He is completely retired. I think he would not feel it is his duty to interfere with what time has now wiped out. If he was still in active service it might be different.'

'It's a terrible story,' said Mrs Oliver, 'terrible. And all those people I talked to – yes, I can see now, they all remembered *something*. Something that was useful in showing us what the truth was, although it was difficult to put together. Except for Monsieur Poirot, who can always put things together out of the most extraordinary things. Like wigs and twins.'

Poirot walked across to where Zélie was standing looking out over the view.

'You do not blame me,' he said, 'for coming to you, persuading you to do what you have done?'

'No. I am glad. You have been right. They are very charming, those two, and they are well suited, I think. They will be happy. We are standing here where two lovers once lived. Where two lovers died and I don't blame him for what he did. It may have been wrong, I suppose it was wrong, but I can't blame him. I think it was a brave act even if it was a wrong one.'

'You loved him too, did you not?' said Hercule Poirot.

'Yes. Always. As soon as I came to the house. I loved him dearly. I don't think he knew it. There was never anything, what you call, between us. He trusted me and was fond of me. I loved them both. Both him and Margaret.'

'There is something I would like to ask you. He loved Dolly as well as Molly, didn't he?'

'Right up to the end. He loved them both. And that's why he was willing to save Dolly. Why Molly wanted him to. Which did he love the best of those sisters? I wonder. That is a thing I shall perhaps never know,' said Zélie. 'I never did – perhaps I never shall.'

Poirot looked at her for a moment, then turned away. He rejoined Mrs Oliver.

'We will drive back to London. We must return to everyday life, forget tragedies and love-affairs.'

'Elephants can remember,' said Mrs Oliver, 'but we are human beings and mercifully human beings can forget.'